* * * * * * *

We had just walked in the door of our apartment when the phone in our office began to ring. I looked at Monica as I set the luggage down, then went to our office to answer the phone. Monica followed me into the office and sat down on one of the chairs while I picked up the receiver.

"McCord Detective Agency, how may I help you?"

"Mr. McCord, this is Russell Larson. Do you remember me?"

"Yes, of course. Your Brandon Smith's chief mechanic, as I recall."

"That's right, at least I was his chief mechanic. Brandon is dead."

At first, I wasn't sure I had heard him correctly, but it quickly soaked in.

"What happened?

"He was murdered."

* * * * * * *

Other titles by J.E. Terrall available at Lulu.com

Western Short Stories
  The Old West*
  The Frontier*
  Untamed Land*
  Tales from the Territory
  Frontier Justice*

Western Novels
  Conflict in Elkhorn Valley*
  Lazy A Ranch
    (A Modern Western)
  The Story of Joshua Higgins*
  The Valley Ranch War*
  Jake Murdock, Bounty Hunter*

Romance Novels
  Balboa Rendezvous
  Sing for Me*
  Return to Me*
  Forever Yours*

Mystery/Suspense/Thriller
  I Can See Clearly*
  The Return Home*
  The Inheritance

Nick McCord Mysteries
  Vol – 1 Murder at Gill's Point
  Vol – 2 Death of a Flower
  Vol – 3 A Dead Man's Treasure
  Vol – 4 Blackjack, A Game to Die For
  Vol – 5 Death on the Lakes
  Vol – 6 Secrets Can Get You Killed

Peter Blackstone Mysteries
  Murder in the Foothills
  Murder on the Crystal Blue
  Murder of My Love
  Murder in the Dark of Night

Frank Tidsdale Mysteries
  Death by Design
  Death by Assassination

Bill Sparks Mysteries
  Murder in the Backcountry*

Non-fiction: Three Brothers Go to War (Letters from WWI)

*Titles also available in Large Print.

MURDER ON THE RACETRACK

VOL 7

A Nick McCord Mystery

by
J.E. Terrall

ISBN: 978-0-9997823-7-8

This is a work of fiction. Names, characters, and incidents are either a product of the author's imagination or are used fictitiously, and any resemblance to actual persons, living or dead, is purely coincidental.

Printed in the United States of America
First Printing / 2020 –www.lulu com

Cover: Front Photo of H.S. Jeffrey's 1954 - 4.9 Mille Miglia Ferrari.
Photo by author, J.E. Terrall

Book layout/
Formatting: J.E. Terrall
                Custer, South Dakota

MURDER ON THE RACETRACK

In memory of H.S. Jeffrey,
a long-time friend who had owned several vintage
race cars during his life, including two Ferraris.
He also shared his passion for vintage race cars,
as well as the sport of sports car racing, with me.

CHAPTER ONE

The flight from New York to Chicago didn't seem to take very long. It might have been due to the fact that both of us were tired and we slept most of the way. Once we were in Chicago, we got our car from the parking structure and headed for home. The drive home took a little over an hour.

When we arrived at our apartment building in Madison, Wisconsin, rather late on Thursday evening, I woke Monica. We gathered our luggage and headed for our apartment.

Monica was feeling pretty good at the moment, but she was still having an upset stomach in the morning. She would feel better after eating something. We had a bit of anxiety about her morning sickness. I think it was more from not being sure of the cause. Monica thought it was probably due to her being pregnant.

We were both tired and needed to get some rest. Since there was nothing we could do tonight to find out about Monica's morning sickness, we decided that the best thing to do was to get some rest and call her doctor in the morning.

Having a doctor check her over might very well put our speculation of the cause of her morning sickness to rest. That being, was she pregnant, or was there some other problem. That's not to say the thought of her being pregnant was a problem. I was even looking forward to the idea of being a father and raising a child even if it meant major changes in our lives. From what Monica had said, she was looking forward to being a mother.

We had just walked in the door when the phone in our office began to ring. I looked at Monica as I set the luggage down, then went to our office to answer the phone. Monica followed me into the office and sat down on one of the chairs while I picked up the receiver.

"McCord Detective Agency, how may I help you?"

"Mr. McCord, this is Russell Larson. Do you remember me?"

"Yes, of course. Your Brandon Smith's chief mechanic, as I recall."

"That's right, at least I was his chief mechanic. Brandon is dead."

At first, I wasn't sure I had heard him correctly, but it quickly soaked in.

"What happened?"

"He was murdered."

"He was murdered?"

"He was racing his vintage 1954 Ferrari roadster when he lost control. He ran into the guardrail and flipped over. He was thrown from the car. The car was heavily damaged. According to the police, he died as a result of the accident. I don't believe the crash was an accident. It shouldn't have killed him."

"What makes you think that?" I asked.

I was curious what it was that made Russell think Brandon should have survived the crash. It was an open cockpit car that left the driver exposed if the car turned over.

"When I looked over the car the evening before the race, everything was fine. There was nothing wrong with it. I think someone must have tampered with the car. I'm also convinced that someone did something to make his seatbelt harness come apart when the car crashed. That's what killed him. The failure of the seatbelt harness."

I heard what sounded like a door closing in the background. I wasn't sure if someone had come into where Russell was calling from, or if someone had just left.

"I gotta run," Russell said quickly, then the phone went dead.

I looked at the phone as I set the receiver down. The first thing that crossed my mind was why did he hang up so quickly. Did someone come into the room he didn't want to hear him talking to me? That seemed like the most logical reason for him to hang up so quickly, but why? Who came into the room, and why was Russell afraid that he might be overheard?

I had no idea what was going on. From the look on Monica's face, she had heard most of what was said and was wondering the same thing.

"That was Russell Larson. He was Brandon Smith's mechanic."

"Is that the same Brandon Smith who is the owner of Smith Metal Fabrication near Calumet City, Illinois, south of Chicago?"

"Yes. How is it you know about him?"

"He, rather his company, did some specialty work for a big display in the museum for the university several years ago. His people did a fantastic job, and donated most of the manhours it took to make and install it. What happened?"

"I don't really know any of the details. Russell hung up before he told me much, but it seems that he thinks Brandon was murdered. Since there isn't much we can do now, I'll start looking into it tomorrow."

I left our office and picked up the luggage. I took our luggage into the bedroom and set it on the foot of the bed.

Monica followed me to the bedroom and stood in the doorway looking at me.

"What's on your mind, Honey?"

"I take it that the police are involved in Brandon's death?"

"Russell said that Brandon died as a result of the accident. Apparently, the police think it was an accident."

"What did the police have to say about it?" Monica asked.

"He didn't really say much, other than to say that the police called it an 'accident'."

"I take it Russell doesn't agree with the police?" she asked.

"No, he doesn't. He hung up on me before he could say very much about it. I got the impression that someone might have come into the room. I'm not sure, but I think I heard a door close in the background. He apparently didn't want whoever came into the room to hear him talking to me."

"What are you going to do?" Monica asked as she looked at me.

"I'm going to take a shower and get some sleep. In the morning, you can call your doctor and get an appointment as soon as possible."

"I mean what are you going to do about Russell's call?"

"Nothing tonight. I'll get a Chicago newspaper in the morning and see if I can find where the race had been held, and what has been reported about the accident. Hopefully, there will be something that will give me an idea of what happened, and if there is a police report on it."

"Will you be going to Chicago to talk to Russell?"

"At this time, I don't know for sure, but probably. I have to find out where Russell is first. The car show was in Chicago, but I don't know where the race was held. I'll try to contact him tomorrow. The number he called from is on our caller ID. I don't see that there is anything I can do tonight," I said.

"Yes, there is," Monica said with a grin. "We can get some rest."

I smiled and agreed wholeheartedly with her. She walked toward me into the bedroom. We began unpacking. Monica helped by sorting those things that needed to be washed from those that could simply be put away. I put the items that could be worn away as she handed them to me. Those things that needed to be washed, she put in a basket to take to the laundry room tomorrow.

As soon as we had everything taken care of, we went into the bathroom. We showered together, but we didn't spend very much time in the shower. We were tired and needed to get some rest.

We had no more than climbed into bed when the phone began to ring again. It was our business phone. I got out of bed and quickly went into the office. I reached over and picked up the receiver as I sat down, hoping that whoever called had not hung up.

"McCord Detective Agency, how may I help you?"

I could hear someone breathing, but they didn't say anything.

"I know you're there and I have your phone number. I suggest you either hang up now or say something."

"Is this Mr. Nick McCord?"

It was a woman's voice, but I couldn't place it.

"Yes, it is. Who is this?"

"Are you the Nick McCord who is a private investigator?"

"Yes," I replied wondering who this woman was and what she wanted.

"I'm Barbara Smith, Brandon Smith's wife. I understand that Russell Larson called you earlier tonight," she said, then paused.

Just hearing her name made me take notice. It crossed my mind that she might have been the one who interrupted Russell's phone call to me.

I looked up at Monica as she stepped into our office.

"Yes, he did. I didn't know your husband very well. I had only met him once or twice, and only briefly. I was sorry to hear that he died while racing his vintage sports car."

"He didn't just die, he was murdered. Someone did something to his car that caused it to crash."

"That is what Russell believes happened."

"That IS what happened. Brandon was too good a driver to have crashed like he did. Someone caused the car to crash. I don't know how it was done, or when it was done, but it was," she said with sharp tone of anger in her voice.

"That car was in perfect condition when it left our garage to go to the antique car show. It was inspected by judges at the show and received a rating of ninety-nine percent perfect. The only flaw they found was one of the small rear taillight lenses was not the one the car should have had. It was a replacement taillight lens."

"I understand. I saw the car several years ago. It was shown at a Concourse De'Alligance Show in Culver City, California. That was where I met your husband. The car was in the show and was judged for being in almost perfect condition to what it was when first built."

"That is correct. It also received a ninety-nine percent perfect rating at that show as well as in Chicago the day before the race," Mrs. Smith said.

"Based on what Russell told me, the police have apparently ruled it an accident. I'm sorry that Brandon died in the accident, but I don't know what I can do for you. I'm assuming that you called me for a reason."

"Yes. I know you are a very good investigator. Both Russell and Brandon had said that you were the best investigator in the area. I would like to know if you could come to the plant in Calumet City and visit with me, personally. I have been told that the police are done examining the car, it will be brought back to Calumet City very soon."

"If the police have already looked at the car and said it was an accident, what do you think I can do?"

"They did say it was an accident, but they didn't do a very thorough inspection of the car. They determined that the front suspension broke and caused the crash, and his seatbelt harness was defective causing him - - - to be thrown - - - from the car. There was nothing wrong with the car, or the seatbelt harness, when he took it out on the track," she insisted.

I could hear her voice catch when she talked about the crash, and her insistence that there was nothing wrong with the car. I was sure that the police were looking into it as an accident, and not as a murder. That was probably because it happened on a closed racetrack during a race. There are often accidents on a racetrack due to faulty equipment, or driver error.

For the police to even look at it at all, someone had to claim it was not an accident. However, if someone called the police and suggested that it had been murder, I had to wonder why they were so quick to conclude it was an accident.

"I don't know what I can do for you, Mrs. Smith. I am not an accident investigator."

I could hear her taking a deep breath. Mrs. Smith sounded as if she thought I could discover who tampered with the car after the show, but before the race, that caused it to crash. I had no idea what I could find by looking at the car.

On the other hand, it would not hurt to look it over. I just might find something that was overlooked. At the very least, I might make her feel better.

"Mrs. Smith, I don't know if I can help or not, but if you want me to look the car over, I would like to have someone there who knows a lot more about that type of car than I do. The best person for that would be Russell."

"I agree. I would be more than willing to pay your expenses and your normal fees if you would come here, talk to Russell and look at the car," she said.

I could hear the sound of hopefulness in her voice. There was no way that I could assure her that I would come to any other conclusion than the police. I could only hope to give her the knowledge that someone had really looked over the car.

"Please, Mr. McCord. Russell told me that if anyone could prove it was not an accident, it would be you. He also said that you were the best private investigator around, and would be straight forward and thorough in your investigation."

"As I said, I'm not an accident investigator, nor am I very knowledgeable about the workings of that kind of car."

"Please, Mr. McCord, would you at least come and look at the car and talk to Russell about it? Please."

I looked at Monica. She had heard most of what was said. She nodded slightly.

"Mrs. Smith, would you mind giving me a minute to confer with my partner?"

"No, not at all. Would you like me to call you back in – say - twenty minutes or so?"

"No. Just give me a couple of minutes."

"Certainly," she said.

After putting my hand over the receiver, I turned to Monica. She had been listening to most of the conversation.

"What do you think?"

"I think you should go see her. What could it hurt? If you determine it was an accident, it might give her at least some piece of mind. If you find the car had been tampered with, she might want you to try to find out who tampered with it and why."

"What about you? I want to be here when you see the doctor."

"Ask her if it would be all right if you go to see her at Calumet City in a couple of days," Monica suggested. "It's only a half a day's drive from here."

"Okay," I said, then I took my hand off the receiver.

"Mrs. Smith?"

"Yes?"

"Would it be all right if I come to Calumet City and meet with you and Russell in a couple of days? I could take a look at it then. I can't guarantee that I can find anything to prove it was anything other than an accident."

"I understand. It would be great to have you look at it. It will take a day or so before we can get the car back to our plant. It's still in the garage at the racetrack. They left it there after they examined it."

"Do you have a place where you can secure the car? I don't want anyone to do so much as wipe the dirt off it. I don't want anyone to do anything at all with it before I have a chance to look it over. That's very important. Do you understand?"

"Yes, I understand. We have a place in the plant where we can put the car and lock it up so no one can so much as touch it."

"Good. Be sure to tell Russell not to do anything with it? I don't want anything done to it before I see it."

"I will, and thank you. I know Brandon thought well of you."

"I'll see you in a couple of days. I'll call you as soon as I'm able to come."

"Thanks again. I look forward to your call and to meeting you. Goodnight."

"Goodnight," I said then hung up.

I walked back to the bedroom with Monica. I didn't have much to say as I was thinking about the call.

As soon as we got back in bed, Monica curled up against me. I was thinking about what happened. Two questions came to mind. Both of them looking at it as murder rather than an accident. Was the 'accident' caused by someone wanting to get Brandon's car out of any further shows by wrecking it, possibly by a jealous competitor who had lost to him? Or was it to get rid of Brandon for some other reason? If it was to get rid of Brandon, who had a reason to get rid of him, and what was the reason? These were all good questions, but with no good answers.

"What are you thinking?" Monica asked as she ran her fingers through the hair on my chest.

"I was just thinking about the accident in the light of it being murder."

"Do you think it was murder?"

"No. I don't know if it was murder or an accident. I was just thinking that if it was murder, who would want Brandon dead?"

"Do you have any ideas who might want him dead?"

"I don't really know. There are always the normal suspects, like someone who would obviously gain by his death. But if it was murder, that opens up the possibility of a number of suspects for any number of reasons. At this time, all I have is Russell thinking it was murder and Brandon's wife telling me it was murder. On the other hand, the police are saying it was an accident."

"I guess you have to go and talk to them. I'm sure you can find something that will show you if it was murder or an accident," Monica said in her usual optimistic way.

I smiled as I pulled her close to me then kissed her. She kissed me back. We took a few minutes just touching and kissing before we curled up together and drifted off to sleep.

CHAPTER TWO

I found myself wide awake just as the sun was coming up. The clock on the bedside table showed it was six-thirty-five. I made every attempt not to wake Monica. She needed to get her rest.

My mind was full of thoughts about the two calls I received last evening which kept me from going back to sleep. The big question was why would someone want to kill Brandon Smith? As far as I knew, he ran his business within the law and was a good, honest businessman who was well-liked and did a lot for the community where he lived.

In my mind, I tried to answer the two big questions. The one I knew nothing about was how well was he accepted into the world of vintage automobiles. Some of the cars were valued at a million dollars, a few of them worth as much as several million. The majority of the vintage cars were owned by very wealthy people. Some of those people might not like a blue-collar working man invading what some might consider an activity for only the elite.

I knew from a friend of mine who had shown his vintage 1953 250 GT Ferrari that the competition to win was often fierce. A few of the wealthy people didn't like to compete against someone from what they considered the "working class", and who just happened to own a vintage or classic automobile regardless of how he got it.

Winning was everything to some of the people who showed their cars. Was it possible that someone was so jealous of Brandon and his rather rare car that they would try just about anything to eliminate him from competition, permanently?

It was likely that if it was jealousy of Brandon and his car, it would most likely be someone who showed cars in the same class as Brandon. However, I knew there was also an overall winner in the form of 'Best of Show', that could greatly add to my list of suspects.

The question was, was jealousy the reason Brandon was murdered? If it was, who would be the one to gain the most from Brandon not being able to show his car? That would be a question that needed to be addressed. Destroying the car would eliminate him from competition, but it wouldn't be necessary to murder him. There was the possibility that the 'accident' was intended to just destroy the car, not to kill the driver.

There was, of course, any number of reasons for someone to want Brandon dead besides something to do with his vintage racing car. It could be someone who didn't like a business deal he or she had made with Brandon. It was also possible that someone got shut out of a business project because Brandon had out bid them. In that case, whoever it was had to have hated him so much that he wanted him dead. Looking into Brandon's business practices might not be a bad idea. Who knows how many enemies he might have made over the years?

What was going through my head was all speculation at this point. I had nothing to go on, but it gave me several ideas that I could work on to see where they might lead. Of course, there was always the possibility that none of them was the reason for his death. It may very well have been someone who didn't like him for some entirely different reason that I knew nothing about, yet.

Then there was also the possibility that it was nothing more than an accident as the police had determined. Whatever the reason for his death, I had two people who were convinced that it was murder. Did either of them stand to gain in some way from his death? That was a possibility I could not overlook. I would have to look into that possibility.

My attention turned to Monica when she moved slightly. I looked over at her and found that she was still sleeping. I began to think about her and what we might find out once she saw her doctor.

The thought of her being pregnant made me think about us and what might have to change in our life style if we were to have a child. For one thing, I would like to have a home with a yard. Kids need a safe place to play.

It would be harder for Monica to go with me while I chase down leads, especially when a case took me out of town, or halfway across the country. I would not like to go alone any more than she would like it. She was my partner and brought a lot of insight into an investigation.

My thoughts were suddenly disturbed when she opened her eyes and saw me watching her. I smiled at her.

"What were you thinking?" she asked.

"I was thinking about us."

"Oh. What about us?"

"I was thinking about how our lives might change if you are pregnant."

"They wouldn't change all that much for at least a little while," she said with her usual optimism.

"Maybe not, but a child to care for would change things."

"I'm sure, but we have time to figure that out. Right now, I would like something to eat."

"What would you like?"

"Big bowl of oatmeal with butter and brown sugar on it," she said with a smile.

"Coming right up, after I get a good morning kiss," I said as I leaned toward her and kissed her.

"How do you feel this morning?"

"I feel like a bowl of oatmeal would make me feel better."

"Coming right up."

"You could have put that a little differently," she said with a slight chuckle in her voice.

"Sorry. I'm on my way to the kitchen. Is that better?"

"Much. Much better."

I got up and slipped into my pants, then left for the kitchen. I immediately started making oatmeal. It wasn't long before she came into the kitchen. She was wearing a robe that fit her figure very nicely.

It didn't take but eight or nine minutes for me to have the oatmeal ready. I got her a glass of juice, then set her bowl of oatmeal on the table and sat down at the table to eat with her. It wasn't long and she smiled at me. I knew she was beginning to feel better.

After we finished breakfast, she went to the phone and called her doctor. I could hear her side of the conversation while I cleaned up the kitchen. She smiled at me when she hung up the phone.

"My doctor said she would fit me in. We have an appointment for nine o'clock."

"We better get ready," I said.

We got ready and I drove her to the doctor's office. We were a few minutes early, but the nurse took her into an examining room right away.

It took about twenty minutes before a nurse came out to the waiting room and asked me to come with her. I followed her into the examining room and found Monica sitting on the examining table. She looked at me. The expression on her face told me that something was wrong.

"What's going on?"

"I'm not pregnant. The test was negative. I'm sorry."

"It's okay, Honey."

"The doctor thinks I have a mild case of stomach flu that just seems to be hanging on. She's running a couple of tests to make sure. I was really hoping I was pregnant," Monica said as tears came to her eyes.

"I was too, but I'm glad we came in."

I stepped up to her and took her in my arms. We held each other while we waited for the doctor to come back.

It was only about ten minutes or so before the doctor came back into the examining room. After a brief introduction, she began to explain what she found out.

"You have a mild case of bacteria in your stomach that irritates your stomach lining. Eating coats the lining of your stomach which is why you feel better after you eat. I'll give you some pills that should put a stop to your upset stomach and get rid of the bacteria."

"How long will it be before I can travel with Nick?"

"I would say about two or three days. It will take about that long before you feel better in the morning," she said.

Monica looked at me. She seemed disappointed.

"Take these pills as directed on the label and you should be fine in two or three days. There are enough pills to last for ten days. Be sure you take them until they are all gone, even if you are feeling fine in the morning. If you still have a problem after you are finished with the pills, give me a call," the doctor said.

We thanked the doctor, then left the doctor's office. Monica didn't say anything until we got to the car.

"I'm sorry. I really wanted to have your baby," Monica said.

"It's okay, Honey. She didn't say anything about you not being able to have a child, did she?"

"No," she said with a slight smile.

I drove her back to our apartment in silence. I guess we didn't really have much to say. All the way back, she rested her hand on my leg while leaning back in the seat with her eyes closed.

When we arrived back at the apartment, we sat down on the sofa and just held each other. It was several minutes before we even talked.

"Honey, I think I'll call Mrs. Smith and tell her it might be a week before I would be able to look over the car."

Monica leaned back and looked at me.

"I think you should call her and tell her you will be there in three days."

"Are you sure?"

"Yes. My doctor said I could travel in two or three days. I want to go with you."

"Are you sure?"

"Yes. We are partners in the agency. I'll be ready to go."

"Okay. I'll call her this afternoon and make sure the car will be there. What do you want to do now?"

"I want you to hold me for a while."

We sat on the sofa for about an hour, just being close. Monica fell asleep with her head on my shoulder. I also drifted off.

The suddenness of the phone ringing in our office woke both of us from our nap. I don't know how long we napped. Monica moved away from me so I could get up and answer the phone. I went into our office and picked up the receiver as I sat down at the desk.

"McCord Detective Agency, how may I help you?"

"Mr. McCord, this is Barbara Smith."

"Hi. I was about to call you. I will be there on Monday shortly after noon. If that's okay with you?"

"That's great. I called to tell you that the car is here at our fabrication plant in Calumet City. I have it secured in a locked area in the plant with instructions that no one is to even go into the room it is in. I didn't even let our people take it off the trailer they used to get it here."

"Very good. Was it your own people who moved the car to the plant?

"Yes. They loaded it on the trailer as soon as the police were done going over it."

"How did it get from the crash site to the police lab?"

"It never went to the police lab. They sent an accident investigator to the racetrack. He looked it over in the garage at the racetrack. Is there a problem with that?" she said sounding worried.

"I thought the police would have taken the car to their lab. It doesn't seem to me that a very good inspection of the car was done under those conditions. It's more important than ever that you don't let anyone touch the car until I get a chance to see it. I also want a list of the names of all the people who helped move that car from the time of the crash to when you secured it."

"I don't know if I can make a list of everyone who had anything to do with the crash, but I'll talk to Russell and get as many names of those who were involved in moving the car as I can. Do you think someone might have tampered with it after the crash?"

"I don't know, I sure hope not."

"I can assure you that I'll have it secured in the room with a lock on the door."

"Good. I will see you in three days. My partner will be with me."

"I can put you and your partner up at my home, if that is acceptable. I have a guest house you can use while you are here."

"That will be fine. I will see you in three days."

"Thank you so much."

"You're welcome. Goodbye," I said, then hung up the phone.

"What now. It sounds like you have everything arranged for our trip to Calumet City," Monica said.

"I think so."

"So, what do we do over the next couple of days?"

"We make sure you get plenty of rest and take your medication as scheduled. I will be doing a bit of research on vintage Ferraris, especially those that are shown at Concours De'Alligance Shows. I want to see if Brandon had any serious competition in his class."

"You think someone might have killed him to eliminate the competition?"

"I don't know, but it is something that should be looked into."

"I agree. I think you have a lot of work to do before we go to Calumet City. I'll leave you to get started."

Monica leaned over and gave me a kiss. She smiled then turned and left the room. She went into the bedroom.

As soon as she was gone, I turned on the computer and waited for it to boot up. As soon as it booted up, I began looking for vintage Ferraris. It took a while, but I was able to find several vintage Ferraris. About all it showed me was there was only one Ferrari like the one owned by Brandon Smith that was known to be in the United States.

I went on to look up any information on Tour De'Alligance Shows around the country. I discovered a number of Ferraris were entered, and a number of those were racing cars. It was the owners of the racing Ferraris I was most interested in.

My next step was to get the names of the participants who had Ferraris entered in the shows where Brandon showed his car before the race. Since that information was not available on the computer site, I hoped I could get it from Barbara Smith.

I made a few notes on what I wanted to talk to Barbara Smith about as well as what I wanted to ask Russell Larson.

Over the next two days, I looked into the business that Brandon had in Calumet City. I didn't find anything there that seemed out of the ordinary or important, but then I didn't have access to his business records; so there was no way to know anything about the financial situation, both his business and personal.

I also got hold of a Chicago newspaper that had a brief article about the accident. It mentioned that police sent an accident investigator to the racetrack, and that the investigator reported that it was "an unfortunate accident that caused the death of the driver of the car". The article also indicated the racetrack played no part in the accident. It was "mechanical failure of the front suspension system of the car that caused the accident", according to the newspaper article.

I wondered how much of an inspection the police had actually done to come up with that decision. Since it was done at the racetrack, and the car had not been taken to a place where it could have been examined more closely, I had my doubts that the car could have been examined very well.

Monica and I spent a lot of time relaxing and getting rested up. I also spent a lot of time thinking about the car and what it might show me.

By the second day of taking her medication, she said she was feeling much better in the morning. She was no longer feeling sick to her stomach.

It was time to pack for the trip to Calumet City and take a look at the car. We would leave in the morning and be there in a few hours.

CHAPTER THREE

It took us a little over three and a half hours to get to Calumet City, Illinois, from Madison. Since it was close to noon when we arrived in the city, we stopped to get something to eat before going to the plant which was located just outside of town.

It was almost one o'clock by the time we finished lunch. The drive from the restaurant to the main gate of the plant took us about fifteen minutes, making it just a little after one o'clock when we arrived. I drove up to the main gate of the Smith Steel Fabrications Company. The gate was closed. We were met by a guard who had been sitting inside the guardhouse. I stopped and waited for the him to stand up and come to me.

"I'm sorry, but the plant is closed today," the guard said.

"I'm Nick McCord. Mrs. Smith is expecting me."

"I'm sorry Mr. McCord, but I still can't let you in."

"Can you call Mrs. Smith and tell her I'm here?"

"She ain't here," he said.

"Then call Russell Larson and tell him I'm here."

"I was told to let no one in. I certainly wasn't told you'd be comin'. Mrs. Smith don't want newspaper people houndin' her," he said rather sharply.

"I'm not a newspaper man, and I'm sure Russell is expecting me. It would be in your best interest to call Russell or Mrs. Smith. I'm sure Russell is somewhere around here since he is expecting me. You understand what I'm telling you?"

The guard looked at me. From the expression on his face, he wasn't sure what he should do.

"You have a phone in the guardhouse, don't you?" I asked rather sharply.

"Yes, sir," he said looking a little nervous.

"Then pick it up and call the office," I insisted.

"Yes, sir."

He hesitated for a moment or two. He must have decided that he had better call. I watched him as he stepped back then turned and went into the guardhouse. I could see him pick up a phone. It was only a couple of minutes before I could see him mouth the words, "yes sir". He quickly hung up the phone then stepped outside.

The guard walked around in front of our car, unlocked the gate and pushed it open. I drove through the gate and drove to the only part of the building that looked like it might be where the offices were located.

After parking the car, I got out and looked around. The parking lot was void of any cars, and there was no one around. I thought that was a little strange since it was a manufacturing business. I couldn't think of one reason why they would shut down the entire plant on a Monday. It wasn't a holiday.

Just as Monica was getting out of the car, I saw Russell come out the door.

"I'm sure glad you could come," Russell said.

"It's good to see you again," I said. "I wish it was under better circumstances."

As we shook hands, he looked past me and saw Monica. He then looked at me and smiled.

"Russell, I would like you to meet my partner and wife, Monica."

"It's nice to meet you, ma'am."

"It's nice to meet you, too," she said with a smile.

"I understand you have Brandon's car here."

"Yeah, what's left of it," he said. "I'll open the garage door. You can drive your car inside."

"What's going on?"

"We are trying to keep a low profile. The news media has been hounding us. They're having a field day with all their speculation about why the plant has been shut down, and what really happened at the vintage car race. I'll explain once we're inside."

I got back in the car while Monica followed Russell into the plant building. It only took a moment before the garage door opened so I could drive in. Once inside, Russell pointed to a place for me to park then closed the garage door.

I parked the car next to what I assumed was Russell's car. As I got out of the car, I got a chance to look around.

In front of where I parked was the plant office. I took a minute to look around. It seemed strange that the big plant was deathly quiet. The large machines stood like motionless giants waiting for someone to wake them up. It gave me an eerie feeling to see the rays of the sun shining down from the windows in the roof and casting shadows on and among the machines. I also noticed that there was no one working in the plant.

"We locked the car up in the large room over in the corner," Russell said.

I looked in the direction he pointed. In the corner of the building there was a white structure that looked like a garage with a large door in the end. I had seen a similar structure that looked like it in an auto repair shop. It was a paint booth where cars were repainted after the damage to them had been repaired.

I walked up to the large door with Russell. Monica walked beside me. While in front of the door, Russell reached into his pocket. He took a key out of his pocket, unlocked the door and then pressed a button. The door began to open.

"Why is the plant closed down. I would think there would be people working."

"Mrs. Smith shut the doors for now. We are moving into a new building. The equipment in this building is going to be sold off. We are having new, more modern equipment installed in our new location next week. Most of our employees are on leave until the new building is ready to use. It will be ready in about ten days."

The way Russell explained the lack of workers seemed logical, but forced. I wasn't sure what was going on, but I was not here to inspect the building. I turned my attention to the open door in front of me.

It was dark in the room. As I stepped up to the opening, I noticed that there were no windows in the room and the only thing I could see was the back of a red car slightly tilted on a trailer.

I heard Russell hit a switch causing the florescent lights that covered the ceiling and the walls from the ceiling to the floor to come on. The lights lit up every square inch of the room. I was a little surprised because it was a paint booth just like those in auto repair shops, only somewhat larger than most paint booths.

"We put the car in here since the building was not in use. It would be secure and there would be lots of light for you while you look it over," Russell said.

"Good thinking. It will be a lot easier to see every bit of the car."

In front of me was a 1954 4.9 millea miglia Ferrari, or what was left of it, on a flatbed trailer. I found myself just standing there looking at it. Russell was kind enough to not say anything. He just let me look at it.

I'm not sure how long I just stood there before Monica moved up alongside me and took hold of my arm. I glanced down at her and saw her looking up at me.

"Are you all right?" she asked.

"Yeah. This is going to take a lot of work. I best get started."

"I'll go to the office and wait for you there."

"Thanks, Honey."

I turned and looked at Russell while Monica walked back to the office.

"Russell, I'll need some tools, and probably some help."

"I've got a large set of metric tools. I'll get them."

"I'll start looking over the car."

I took a few minutes to slowly walk around the car. I was looking for something that would give me an idea of where I wanted to start looking for possible evidence. Something that might tell me what happed just before the car crashed. It wasn't until I got to the left front corner of the car, that something caught my attention. It was hard to miss.

The left front wheel was hanging loose on the car and had apparently been ripped from its mounting points on the frame. It seemed the only thing holding the wheel to the car was the brake line. I couldn't be a hundred percent sure, but this may have been the cause of the accident. It could also be the result of what happened when it crashed. I was sure the police investigator thought the same thing.

Just then, Russell returned wheeling in a rather large tool chest. He walked over to me and looked at the front of the car.

"Do you think you found something?"

"I might have. I'm going to need coveralls."

"I doubted that you would bring some with you. You will find a pair in the office. There's a bathroom inside the office where you can change."

"Thanks. Don't touch anything," I reminded him.

"No problem. I'll wait outside by the door so no one else comes in here."

I thought about what he said as I walked to the office. His comment about others coming in struck me as strange since I had not seen anyone in the building but the three of us, although there might have been others in the building. It was a rather large building, and someone could be working on something in the back of the building without us knowing.

As soon as I made a quick change into the overalls, I started back toward the front of the car. There was a new pair of gloves in the pocket of the coveralls. I put them on as I walked back to the car.

I started by taking a good number of pictures before I did anything else. I then spent the next hour or so carefully taking the wheel and its suspension assembly off the car, trying to see any abnormalities in the parts as I removed them. I noticed that three of the steel bolts that held the wheel to the suspension assembly were broken off at the contact point. Only the head of the bolts and a short piece of the shaft were where I could see them. In my search of the car and trailer, I was unable to find the lower part of the bolts where the nut would be. The lower part of each of the bolts were missing.

My first thought was this was the cause of the accident, it certainly would have caused the car to crash. Having only the upper part of three bolts still in the holes led me to think that the lower parts of the bolts were probably somewhere on the racetrack, but a close look around was still a good idea.

I immediately began looking for the other parts of the bolts, as well as anything else that might have contributed to the crash. I looked over the undercarriage but didn't find them. However, I did find a fourth bolt. It was easy to see that it was the same size, but a different kind of bolt than the others. I was able to find both ends of the fourth bolt.

I quickly discovered the fourth bolt looked like it might have been tampered with, but it would take a metallurgy lab to tell me for sure. Hopefully, they would be able to tell me what part of the car the bolt had come from. It didn't look like it was part of the suspension system, and I couldn't find where it had come from.

"I take it you found something," Russell said.

"Yes, I did. Do you know what part of the car this bolt came from? I found it lying on the deck of the trailer right under the edge of the frame of the car."

I held it up for Russell to look at. He took it from my hand and looked it over good before he looked at me.

"I don't know where it came from. The markings on it sure indicate that it belongs to a Ferrari."

"Do you know what part of the car it's from?"

"No. I can't even say for sure it's from this car."

Russell's last comment caused me to think about it. If it was not from this car, where was it from and how did it get there?

"Was this trailer used to haul any other car at any time?"

"No. As far as I know, this trailer was never used to haul anything by this car."

I decided that all the bolts needed to be examined by a metallurgist who knows his business. I happen to know there is a professor in the School of Engineering at the University of Wisconsin who just might be able to help me.

"I'm going to take these bolts to a lab in Wisconsin to have them examined. I want to know everything there is to know about them."

"You think the bolts might have been tampered with in some way to cause the car to crash?" Russell asked.

"Maybe. I don't know if it will help or not, but it is evidence. In fact, the whole car is evidence."

Russell handed the bolt to me. He watched me as I wrapped both of the partial bolts and the odd bolt in a shop rag, then put them in my pocket. I didn't want anything to happen to them.

"Do you think the bolts were the cause of the accident?" Russell asked.

It struck me as strange that he asked almost the same question twice. He seemed a little too interested in my interest in the bolts. It caused me to think that he might know more than he was telling me.

"Probably, but I won't know until I have a lab check them out. I'm still not sure it is the cause of the crash that took Brandon's life. The crash might have caused the front suspension to break away from the frame, rather than the suspension breaking away causing the accident."

"What makes you think that?"

"It's mostly just a guess on my part. Did Brandon die in the car?"

"No, he was thrown from the car when it rolled over."

"Brandon wasn't wearing a seatbelt harness? Why wasn't Brandon wearing a seatbelt harness?"

"He was. I helped strap him in," Russell said.

"Then why was he thrown from the car?"

"The police said that his harness must have broken. The violence of the crash probably caused the harness to break."

"Being thrown from the car was probably due to the violence of the crash causing the harness to fail, is that what you're telling me?"

"That's what the police said?"

"What do you think?" I asked.

"I don't know, but the harness looked fine when I helped Brandon into it."

I took a minute to look at the car. It was hard for me to think that the seatbelt harness would have failed, not that it was impossible. From the look of it, it was a new harness. I decided that I would take the seatbelt harness off the car and have it examined closely. I also wanted to see if it had been properly attached to the car.

Once I had examined how the seatbelt harness had been attached to the car, and the fact that it was still attached to the car; I couldn't see anything to make me believe it had not been attached properly. The next thing was to have the catch examined by someone who could tell me if the catch had been tampered with.

Before I removed the seatbelt harness, I took several pictures of it. I then carefully put it in a box. I would personally take it to a man I knew who would be able to examine it and tell me everything I would want to know about it.

After I had the seatbelt harness secured in the box, I went to office and gave it to Monica. I returned to the car and continued to look over the Ferrari. As I did, I took a good number of photos of the car, inside and out, and where I removed parts for further examination.

After working on the car for several hours, I found a dark spot on the floorboard of the car. At first, I thought it might be a blood spot, but that didn't seem logical if Brandon had been thrown from the car. I got a piece of paper and carefully scraped a little of the dark material off the floor and onto the paper. I carefully folded it up so the sample would not fall out, then placed it in my pocket.

Once I was finished with my examination of the car, I sat down with Russell in the office. I asked Russell a lot of questions about the car's history. I wanted to know who had owned the car before Brandon got hold of it, and who did the restorations work on the car after Brandon bought it.

As soon as I had all the information on the car I felt I could get from Russell, I told him to lock up the car and keep everyone away from it. He nodded that he understood.

As soon as he left the office to lock up the car, I placed a call to Barbara Smith at her home.

"Hello," a male voice said.

"Who am I speaking to?"

"My name is Josh, Mrs. Smith's Personal Assistant."

"I'm Nick McCord. Is Mrs. Smith available to speak to me?

"Yes, Mr. McCord. Just one moment."

It didn't take long for Barbara to answer the phone.

"Hello, Mr. McCord. Are you finished examining the car?"

"Yes, at least for now."

"Is it good news?"

"At this point, it is hard to say. I still have much more to do. I would rather not discuss it on the phone."

"I understand. Since you and your wife will be staying in my guest house here at the estate, why don't the two of you come and have dinner with me here?"

"That's very nice of you. I can explain things then. We will be there in about thirty minutes. Would that be okay?"

"That would be fine. Please come to the back gate. It seems the news media is getting rather pushy at the front gate. It seems someone on my staff apparently leaked it out that Brandon was murdered. Up until that came out, it was considered to be an accident and the media didn't take much interest in it."

"That's probably a good idea. Be sure to let your guard at the rear gate know we are coming in that way."

"I will," she said then hung up.

I looked over at Monica. I could tell by the look on her face that she was wondering what was going on.

"I think we are done here for now. Mrs. Smith has invited us to dinner."

"Are we still staying at her place?"

"Yes, but from the sounds of it, we will be staying in the guest house."

I glanced over at Russell. He was just standing there looking at us. I don't know why, but I got the impression that he was concerned about something. Was he afraid that I had found something on the car, but didn't want to say anything about it? Or did he have something to say to me, but wasn't sure if he should.

"I'll get out of these coveralls then we can go," I said to Monica.

I took the box containing the seatbelt harness with me into the bathroom. As soon as I changed, I made sure that I had the bolts and the box with the seatbelt harness in it, in my hands. When I came out of the bathroom, I noticed that Russell was looking at what I was carrying.

"I can lock those things up here in the safe until you're ready to take them for testing," Russell said.

"I think I'll keep them with me. I don't want the chain of custody broken. They could prove to be evidence, if a crime had been committed. If they prove not to be anything related to the crash, I'll let you have them."

"Do you think it was not an accident?" Russell asked.

"I don't know. I hope once these items are examined, I will know."

Russell didn't say anything more. He simply turned around and walked out of the office.

As we left the plant, I glanced over toward the paint booth. Russell was standing in the door looking at the car. I wondered what was going through his mind. I was beginning to have some serious concerns about him. It was almost as if he knew something about the crash, but was not going to tell me about it.

I walked with Monica to the door, but paused at the door for a minute to watch Russell. When he finally shut off the lights and pressed the button that closed the door on the paint booth, I turned and followed Monica out the door to the car.

I thought about Russell while I got in the car. The look on Russell's face and his actions during the examination of the car, caused me to think that it might not be a good idea to trust him too much. At least until I knew him better. If I was honest with myself, he would have to be one of my suspects if it turned out that foul play was involved in Brandon's death. In fact, anybody who had access to the car from the time of the show to the race would be suspect. He certainly would have been one of those who had access to the car, and the knowledge to fix the car so it would crash.

"What are you thinking?" Monica asked.

"I'm a little concerned about Russell."

"Do you think he had something to do with the accident?"

"Not really. There's something about his actions that don't seem to be what I would expect. It's almost as if he is hiding something from me."

"Maybe it is a good idea to keep what you found out about the car to ourselves, and not say much to him, or anyone else, until we are sure."

"That is what I plan to do," I said.

I reached down and started the car. We left the plant and headed for the Smith Estate.

CHAPTER FOUR

It was about twenty-five minutes after leaving the plant when I turned into the back gate to the Smith Estate. I noticed several people milling around as if they were waiting for something. When I got closer, it was easy to see that they were news people from a couple of the local news outlets. There were two men who had video cameras and two other people with mics in their hands. At least three others looked like they might be newspaper reporters.

As I pulled to a stop, one of the men with the video cameramen came toward me. When I stepped out of the car, he came up to me. There was a woman who had a mic in her hand next to him. I stepped closer to the cameraman and put my hand over the lens of his camera.

"You are on private property, therefore you are trespassing. If you don't leave this property immediately, I will have you arrested," I said looking at the woman with the mic in her hand, ready to stick it in my face.

She looked at me for a moment trying to figure out if I really could have them arrested, then she looked at the cameraman. She nodded at the cameraman. He lowered his camera and backed off a little, but the woman with mic did not back off.

"Don't press your luck, lady," I said.

I looked her right in the eyes. She took a second or two before she backed away with her cameraman.

I turned to the others and said, "You can all leave now. No one here is going to talk to you or make any comments. If any of you trespass on this property again, I will call in a couple of police units to take you to jail."

"You can't do that. We're from the press," one of them yelled.

"Being from the press doesn't protect you from being arrested for trespassing, or harassing people who are lawfully going in or out of this residence. Now move it."

I stood there looking at them. It only took a few seconds before they started pulling back, then began walking down the drive to the curb at the street.

I turned around and went back to my car. The guard at the gate just stood there looking at me. I walked over to him. I noticed he was grinning.

"I'm Nick McCord. Mrs. Smith is expecting me."

"Thanks for making them move away from the gate."

"No problem. By the way what is your name?"

"Neal Upton."

"Well, Neal, don't hesitate to call the police if they trespass again."

"I won't. I'll open the gate for you, Mr. McCord."

I got back in the car and drove through the gate. It was a fairly long drive up to the house and around to the front entrance. When we arrived at the front of the house, a rather tall, good looking young man in a dark suit stepped out onto the porch.

"Is that Barbara's personal assistant?" Monica asked.

"I don't know. It could be, but he looks more like a body guard to me."

"She has good taste in men. He looks more like a male model to me."

"We'll soon find out who he is and what he's doing here."

I opened the car door and got out. I walked around the car and opened the door for Monica. I held her hand as we stepped up on the porch.

"Good afternoon. I'm Josh Ellis. I'm Mrs. Smith's personal assistant. She is waiting for you in her office. This way, please."

As we followed him into the house, Monica glanced up at me. I had a pretty good idea what she was thinking.

We went down a rather long hall then turned and entered an office. Mrs. Smith was sitting behind a rather large desk. The high backed, black leather chair looked almost like a throne and she was the queen.

She looked up, then stood up when she saw us come into the office behind Josh. She was rather tall and wore a tailored dress with a lot of jewels around her slender neck. There was no doubt that she was a very striking woman, and she looked like a woman of wealth.

I couldn't help but think that it might very well be a front. At this point I had no idea why I thought that except for the fact she appeared to be dressed to impress someone. If it was me, I was not all that impressed.

"This is Mr. Nick McCord and his wife, Monica," Josh said.

"Welcome to my home. It is so nice to finally meet you."

"This is a very lovely home," Monica said.

"Yes, it is, isn't it," she replied as she looked around the room as if it was all new to her.

"We understand that we are staying in your guest house. It has been a rather busy day for us. Would it be too much to ask you to have someone show us to the guest house so we could freshen up before dinner?" I asked.

"Not at all, Mr. McCord. Josh will show you to your quarters. Dinner will be ready by … six-thirty? Would that be satisfactory?"

"That would be fine, and thank you."

"Josh, would you show them to the guest house, please."

"Yes, ma'am. Right this way."

Josh led us down a long hall and into the dining area. I noticed that Monica had been looking at the paintings on the wall and at the small tables with different small pieces of art such as vases and small statues. I also noticed that she didn't comment on any of them.

As we passed through the dining room, I noticed a rather large picture of a woman sitting on a fancy French style chair of what appeared to be from the sixteenth century. I only knew about the chair because our last case dealt with a lot of antique furniture. I had seen several chairs like it at the time.

We were led out of the dining room onto a rather large stone patio. At one end of the patio was what looked like a small house. It was built of the same basic materials that had been used in the big house. We walked up to it and Josh opened the door.

"This is our guest house. We hope that you will be comfortable here. Mrs. Smith thought you might be more comfortable staying here rather than in the main house. It would provide you with more privacy, and give you a place to work without anyone bothering you."

"That was very thoughtful of her," I said.

"There is a garage at the back of the guest house. If you would like, I would be happy to bring your car around and park it in the garage. You would have easier access to your luggage and you wouldn't have to bring it through the house."

"That's very nice, but I'll go get our car if you don't mind. It's been a long drive and I would like to stretch my legs a bit."

"Of course. In that case, I'll leave you to get settled in. If you should need anything, just pick up the phone and dial 3. .I will answer any questions you might have, or get anything you might need," he said.

He reached out and handed me the key to the guest house. I thanked him, then he turned and left.

I watched him as he left the guest house. I couldn't get over the feeling that things were not what they seemed. Maybe it was my suspicious nature from being lied to by clients, and having them not telling me what I needed to know.

"This is really very nice," Monica said.

She turned to look at me and stopped suddenly when she saw me with my finger in front of my lips.

"Would you like to take a little walk with me to get the car? It will give you a chance to stretch your legs a little."

"Sure. I'd like that," she said.

I took her by the hand. We left the guest house and started around the outside of the main house to the front where we had left the car. We had not gotten very far when Monica spoke to me.

"Did you see all the fancy French furniture in the hall? All those small tables displaying different pieces of art?"

"Yes. What about them?"

"Those tables are not French at all. They are fake, or better put, reproductions of the real thing. I would guess that the art work in most of this house is fake as well, but I can't be sure without a closer look at it.

"I also got a peek into a couple of the rooms as we walked by them. The doors to the rooms were open slightly. In one room I was able to see in, it had very little in the way of furniture. What furniture I could see in the room was all relatively new furniture, and not real cheap stuff, but certainly not the most expensive, either," Monica said.

"In another room I was able to see in, it didn't look like there was any furniture at all. I think someone is trying to make it look like they have money, and lots of it. Based on what I have seen so far, I would guess they are broke, or very close to it."

"I have to agree. By the way, what was the look you gave me when we first entered the house behind Josh?" I asked.

"Oh. I was wondering what 'assistance' he was providing Barbara."

"That's what I thought you were thinking," I said with a smile. "Did you take a good look at the guest house? It looks more like a servant's quarters."

"It would be my guess it was a servant's quarters at one time."

"I have to wonder what is going on here. Why the air of wealth? Who are they trying to impress?" I said.

"I noticed that the plant was empty. It didn't look like anyone had worked there for sometime," Monica said.

"I noticed that as well. There was a lot of dust on the floor and on the machines. I don't think that plant has been used for long time."

"Do you think Brandon might have been killed for his life insurance?"

"What made you think of that?" I asked.

"The front they seem to be putting on. That, and the fake antique furniture. All that makes me think they are not as well off as they would like us to believe. Maybe they need money."

"It's possible. I think it would be a good idea to look into Brandon's financial situation."

"How did he maintain his business if the plant has not been working for a long time?" Monica asked. "Do you think he might have another plant somewhere? Maybe a smaller plant?"

"I was told they were moving to a new plant in the next week or so. The machinery in the old plant is going to be sold off. According to Russell, the new plant is to have all new modern equipment and be ready to use next week to ten days. Their employees are on leave until the new plant is ready to use, according to Russell."

"Do you think you were told the truth?" Monica asked.

I had to think about what she was saying. If he had a new plant and it wasn't in operation yet, why was the old plant setting idle? Something was going on here. It just didn't smell right.

"The reason I didn't want you to say anything in the guest house is I'm not sure if it is bugged. With so many things that don't seem to add up, I didn't want to take the chance that everything we say, they hear," I said.

"We best get the car and our luggage to the guest house before they get suspicious," Monica said.

We got in the car and drove it around from in front of the main house to the guest house garage at the back of the main house. Once we had it parked in the garage, we took our luggage inside the guest house.

We quickly got ready for dinner, then walked across the patio and entered the dining room. The first thing I noticed was the table had been set for five. I knew there were three of us, Barbara Smith, Monica and myself. I was a bit curious who the other two might be. I thought that Josh was probably one of them. Maybe Russell was going to join us. I guess I would just have to wait to find out.

It was only a few minutes after we entered the dining room when Barbara came into the room with Josh.

"Please sit down. It will be a few minutes before our other guest will be here. He was delayed by traffic. He is on his way from Chicago. I'm sure you have a lot to tell me about what you found when you examined Brandon's car." Barbara said hopefully.

"I don't really have a lot to say at this time."

"But I'm sure you do have something to tell me after working on the car all afternoon," Mrs. Smith said.

"Yes. I did find several broken bolts from the front suspension system, and a bolt that I have been unable to find out where it came from. I am going to take them to the University of Wisconsin's Engineering Department to be examined to see if they simply broke, or if they had been tampered with in some way."

"Do you think that these – ah – bolts – may have caused the accident?"

"There is no way for me to tell without having them examined by experts."

I did notice that she was now calling it an accident. She had been so sure that it was murder when I first talked to her on the phone.

"Is that all you found, Mr. McCord?" Josh asked.

"No. I believe that his seatbelt harness failed during the accident."

"The police were able to tell us that much," Josh said.

"Yes, I know, but I want to see if it simply failed, or if it was tampered with to make sure it failed."

"I see," Barbara said as he looked at Josh.

I noticed the exchange of glances between Josh and Barbara. I couldn't say for sure what it meant, but there was something going on between them.

I was about to ask her about the empty plant with all its machinery when I heard someone come into the dining room. I turned to see who it was.

A tall well-built man in his mid-fifties walked into the room. He was dressed in what appeared to be an expensive dark gray pinstriped suit. He walked up to Barbara and leaned down and kissed her on the cheek. She smiled up at him.

"Mr. McCord, this is Mr. Moorhouse. He is a lawyer from Chicago. He is my lawyer and handles much of my business affairs.

"George, this is Nick McCord and his lovely wife, Monica. They are very well-known investigators from Madison, Wisconsin. They are here to find out if Brandon's death was an accident or murder."

"It is nice to meet you. I have heard of you, Mr. McCord. You have a reputation for solving crimes."

"I do try," I said.

"Don't be so modest. You are good at what you do."

"Shall we eat," Barbara interrupted. "We can talk about the accident after dinner."

The talk almost immediately turned to a lot of small talk during dinner. Mr. Moorhouse seemed to be interested in my background in law enforcement. He asked several questions that caused me to wonder what it was he was really trying to find out. It was easy to see that he was probably a very good defense lawyer.

Monica seemed to be getting drilled by Barbara. I knew Monica was quite able to handle herself, even under pressure. It didn't sound like Barbara was getting much information out of her. However, it did sound like Monica was getting a feel for what was going on in Barbara's head without Barbara realizing it. Monica had a very disarming way about her. People would tell her things they might not tell anyone else.

After dinner we all retired to the sitting room near the front door of the house.

"Well, Mr. McCord, how is your investigation going? I understand that you have looked at the car?" Mr. Moorhouse asked.

"That is correct."

"Did you find anything interesting?"

"Not so far."

"Oh. I was told you found some broken parts of the car."

"I did."

"What were they?"

"A few broken bolts."

"What do they have to do with the accident?"

"I don't know."

"Certainly, you can speculate on them."

"I'm not in the business of speculating. I'm in the business of dealing in facts. Just like you're in the business in dealing with laws."

"In other words, you're not going to tell me what happened," George said with a hint of frustration in his voice, and maybe a little anger.

"I'm not going to even tell you what I think might have happened until I know what happened," I said while looking him right in the eyes.

"Gentlemen, this is a friendly gathering," Barbara said. "And George, you of all people should know that a good investigator doesn't deal in guesses."

"I'm sorry. I guess I got a little carried away. I had a tough day in court today. I hope you will except my apology, Mr. McCord."

"No problem. We all get a little 'carried away'. as you put it, from time to time," I said with a slight grin.

"What I would like to know is do you think you might have a clue to what happened?" Josh asked.

"At this time, I would have to say no, not really. I do hope to have some idea of what happened after some tests are run on a couple suspicious items I found. However, I do not wish to talk about them at this time since I don't know if they have anything to do with the accident."

"Well, I guess we will just have to wait," Josh said as he looked from Barbara to George.

I looked at Josh when he turned and looked at Barbara. The look in her eyes and her body language gave me the impression that she didn't like how things were going. The fact that I didn't tell them anything seemed to upset both Barbara and George. It was a time for me to be very careful what I said, even if I found something that had nothing to do with anything.

It was getting late. I decided that it was time to excuse ourselves and turn in. I stood up and reached out to Monica.

"I hope you will excuse us. It has been a long day for us. We can talk tomorrow before we go back to Madison in the morning, if you wish."

"Certainly. We will have breakfast for you in the sunroom before you go," Barbara said. "If you need anything, just call."

"I think we have everything we need," I said.

"Goodnight, and thank you for a very good dinner and pleasant conversation," Monica said.

We left the others and returned to the guest house. I glanced back and saw what looked like a possible heated discussion between Barbara, George, and Josh. I wondered if it was about what I had told them, or more to the point, what I didn't tell them.

Once Monica and I were in the guest house, I went to the garage and retrieved the box with the bolts and the seatbelt harness, and took them into the guest house. I took the bolts and the seatbelt harness out of the box and placed them under a chair that had a skirt that hung all the way to the floor. I put a book in the box and set it on the dresser across the room from the bed. After lining up one edge of the box with a couple of lines on the dresser, I walked across the room to the bed.

Monica smiled at me, but didn't say anything. We got ready for bed then turned in without saying a word. I kissed her goodnight then we curled up together.

CHAPTER FIVE

I woke early. I'm not sure why. Maybe it was because I thought I heard something in the garage. I smiled at the thought of the box that had been in the car, but was not in the car now. For someone to search the car was a waste of time and effort. However, I was curious about who might want to make sure that the items I took off the Ferrari would never make it to the lab for examination. What were they afraid the lab might discover if they were examined, or did they already know what the lab would find?

My thoughts were disturbed by Monica. She rolled over and looked at me.

"Is it time to get up?"

"No. You can sleep a little longer," I said.

"How long have you been awake?"

"Not very long."

"Are you ready to get up?"

"Yes," I said as I put my fingers over my mouth.

I leaned down close to Monica and whispered in her ear.

"I think we should get out of here as soon as you are ready. Someone was in the garage. I suspect they were looking for the box. No telling what they might do because it wasn't there."

"Do you know who it was?" Monica asked in a whisper.

"No, but if I had to guess, it was probably Josh. I got the impression that Barbara and her lawyer were a little too interested in what I found and what I plan to do with it. Josh seems to be the one that Barbara would have do her dirty work."

"I'll get dressed," Monica whispered.

I got out of bed and began getting dressed while Monica went into the bathroom. When she came out, she was dressed and ready to go.

"How are you feeling this morning?"

"I'm fine. I'm hungry, but not because my stomach is upset," she said then leaned toward me and whispered. "I can wait to get something to eat if you want to get out of here."

"I think we should get out of here as soon as possible. I don't want to let the box out of my sight. I do however, want to check out our car to make sure nothing was done to it during the night," I whispered.

"I'll wait here with the evidence box while you check out the car."

I nodded. After I put the items to be examined back in the box. I went to the door to the garage. After glancing at Monica, I listened at the door. When I didn't hear anything, I reached out and slowly turned the door knob. Carefully, I opened the door, then looked out into the garage. I didn't see anyone.

Since it was all clear, I left the guest house and entered the garage to check on the car. It was easy to see that someone had searched the car. The car blanket on the backseat was not where it had been when I took the box off the floor behind the driver's side seat yesterday evening.

After making sure there was no one around who could see what I was doing, I started by looking under the dash for anything that didn't belong there, such as a tracking device. I found nothing. I checked the inside of the car including under the seats and in the door panels and found nothing.

However, a look under the car did produce results. I had to smile at the clumsy attempt to put a miniature tracking device under the rear bumper where it would not be found. It's often the first place a person usually hides such a gadget. It's also the first place people who know about such things would look.

My first thought was to remove it from the car, but decided that if I left it under the bumper, I might discover who planted it. I continued to look the car over just in case they had put a second tracking device on the car in case I found one. I found nothing else that should concern us.

Since the tracking device was completely self-contained and did not rely on power from the car, I came up with an idea. I would remove the tracking device from under the rear bumper and put it inside the car. At some point along the way, I would drop it off then change my route to Madison.

After putting the tracking device in the backseat of the car, I returned to the guest house. We gathered up our belongings and the evidence. We put them in the car and drove off the property.

As soon as we were well on our way, I told Monica about the tracking device and what I did with it. She seemed a little concerned, but didn't say anything.

Once out on the road, I continued to watch for someone who might be following us at a distance. I didn't see anyone who looked like they were going to follow us until we were several miles from the estate.

We had just turned onto the Interstate when I saw a car behind us that looked like one I had seen at the Smith Estate when we arrived yesterday. I wasn't a hundred percent sure, but it was worth keeping an eye on.

"Keep an eye on that blue car in the left-hand lane," I said.

"You think that is the car that is following us."

"Yes. I saw the car parked a couple of blocks from the Smith Estate. It pulled out after we went a couple of blocks, then followed us onto the interstate."

As I cruised along the interstate at the posted speed limit, I watched the car in my rearview mirror. Traffic was not real heavy at this hour which made it easier to keep an eye on the car even though he was some distance behind us. Unfortunately, it also made it easy for them to keep an eye on us.

Monica had been watching the car behind us in the side rearview mirror. We had not talked for some time. She turned and looked at me. From the look on her face, she seemed to be asking me if it was safe to talk."

"It's safe to talk. The tracking device was not the type of bug that would allow them to hear us. What's on your mind?"

"Are you going to let them follow us all the way to Madison?"

"No. The longer they follow us, without us doing anything other than just drive along, the less likely they are to think we know they are there."

"But once they are comfortable, you will ditch them, right?"

"Not only beautiful, but smart, too."

Monica smiled then reached over and put her hand on my leg. I reached down and patted her hand.

"How do you plan to ditch them?"

"I haven't worked it out just yet, but I'll think of something. The problem is they are so far behind me and the traffic is light."

"How is that a problem?"

"It makes it harder for me to tie them up in traffic while we disappear."

"Oh."

Monica didn't say anything more. She sat looking out the side window at the rearview mirror.

I suddenly came up with an idea.

"Are you ready to get something to eat?" I asked.

"Sure. Did you have something in mind?"

"There's a truck stop a couple of miles up ahead. We can get something to eat there."

"Okay."

"I want you to see if you can reach the tracking device in the backseat."

Monica looked at me for a second before she unhooked her seatbelt. I kept an eye on the car following us while she retrieved the tracking device, then turned around, sat back down and buckled up again.

"I take it you have a plan."

"I sure do."

We were just coming up on the exit ramp that would take us to the truck stop. I got off the interstate then drove to the truck stop. As soon as I parked the car, I stepped out of the car and looked over the top of it. I could see the car following us had pulled into the truck stop. It pulled into a parking space some distance from where I had parked. I walked around and opened the door for Monica.

"Don't look now, but our tail just parked a few rows away from us," I said as I opened the car door.

I reached out and took Monica's hand as she got out of the car.

"You have the tracking device?"

"Yes. I have it in my purse. Should I leave it in the car?"

"No. I doubt they will be paying any attention to it as long as our car is parked where they can see it."

We walked into the café at the truck stop and sat down near a window that would allow us to look out over the parking lot. I could see our car, but couldn't see the car that I thought had been following us.

"Monica, can you see the car that was following us?"

"Yes. There are two men in the car. They are just sitting there."

Just then the waitress came up to our table. We took a minute to order our breakfast. As soon as the waitress left for the kitchen with our order, I looked at Monica.

"One of them is getting out of the car. He's walking toward our car. Now he is standing next to our car and looking around."

I quickly stood up and ran out of the café. As I ran toward the car, the man who had been standing next to our car saw me. He quickly turned and took off running.

When I got to our car, I noticed that he had left behind a pry bar normally used to break into a car. He was too far ahead of me for me to catch him, but I did get a fairly good look at him as he jumped into the car that had been following us.

I watched them as they sped out of the parking lot. With all the cars in the parking lot, I was unable to get a license plate number, but I was sure it was an Illinois plate.

I turned and looked at the pry bar. There was little doubt in my mind that it would have any useable fingerprints on it, but I would have it checked to be sure. I picked it up using a handkerchief so I would not destroy any fingerprints that might be on it and I would not leave my fingerprints on it.

After unlocking the trunk, I placed the pry bar in the trunk so it wouldn't roll around, then locked the car. As soon as I felt the car was secure again, I returned to the café for breakfast.

I sat down just as my breakfast arrived. We didn't talk about what happened, but I was thinking about it and who might be involved. There was something going on and there was little doubt in my mind that it involved Josh, and probably Mrs. Barbara Smith.

"What are you thinking?"

"I'd rather wait until we are in the car and on the road again."

"Okay."

When we had finished our breakfast, I took Monica by the hand as we walked to the car. I held the door for her. Once she was in the car, I asked her for the tracking devise. She looked at me for a second, then handed it to me.

I walked over to a car just a couple of cars away from our car. After looking around, I walked behind the car, bent down and slipped the tracking devise under the rear bumper.

After checking again to see if anyone had seen me, I returned to our car. I got in and sat down behind the wheel, but didn't start the car.

"Are we waiting for someone?"

"Yes. I'm waiting for the couple who came in that car. They had breakfast in the booth behind us. I heard them talking. It seems they are going to Chicago."

"You are sneaky. You're hoping that those two men who had been following us will follow them."

"I just hope they don't discover that they are following the wrong car before we have a chance to lose them.

"You think they will try again to get the box of evidence?"

"I would have to say, yes. They must think it will prove that Brandon's car was tampered with, or they wouldn't go to such measures to prevent us from getting it to the lab for testing."

We sat quietly for only about fifteen minutes before the couple came out of the café. They got in the car and drove away. I waited for another five minutes or so before I started our car and drove out onto the interstate.

As soon as I was sure that we were not being followed, I turned off the interstate and headed west on a secondary highway. Monica was watching the side rearview mirror. I was also watching out the rearview mirror from time to time to make sure we had lost them. We didn't see them again.

We arrived at the Wisconsin University Campus a little after one. I drove directly to the College of Engineering at Wisconsin University. I found a parking place near the building.

I looked around to make sure we were not in any danger of someone having beaten us here before I opened the car door. While Monica got out of the car, I retrieved the box from the back seat. We hustled into the building then walked down the hall to the office of Professor Jonathan F. Houzerman. I knew the professor to be a very good metallurgist from a case I worked on when I was a Milwaukee Police Detective.

I looked up and down the hall before I opened the door to the professor's office. Once inside, I saw the professor's secretary look up and smile.

"May I help you?"

"I'm here to see Professor Houzerman."

"Do you have an appointment? I don't see one on his schedule."

"No, but it is a matter of some importance. Would you be so kind as to tell him that Nick McCord is here to see him?"

"One moment, please."

I watched the woman get up and go into the professor's office. It was only a matter of a moment or two before the professor came out of his office with his secretary right behind him.

"Detective McCord, it is so nice to see you again."

"It is good to see you, too," I said as we shook hands.

"What brings you to my humble office? I take it the police need a little help with something?"

"First of all, I should tell you that I am no longer with the Milwaukee Police Department. I'm a private investigator now."

"Oh. I didn't know that. No matter, what can I do for you? I take it you have something you want me to look at since you have a box in your hands."

"Yes, I do."

"And does it have something to do with Professor Monica Barnhart?" he asked as he looked at her and smiled. "It is nice to see you again, Monica. How have things been going with you since you left the University?"

"Very well. Thank you, and it's Doctor Monica McCord now," she said with a smile.

"Oh. Congratulations."

"Thank you," Monica said.

"I have some items I would like you to look at and tell me if they have been tampered with in some way," I said as I handed him the box. "Since I am not with the police department, I will be paying for your services."

"Fine. Come into my office. We'll take a look at them and decide what steps need to be taken from there."

I simply nodded and followed Monica and the professor into his office.

Professor Houzerman set the box on a table, then opened it. He removed all the items in the box and spread them out on the table.

"Well, what do we have here? It looks like four bolts, three of which are broken, and a seatbelt harness. Do you have the other parts of the broken bolts?"

"No. I was unable to find the other half. I would like you to tell me everything you can about them," I said.

"I would like to have the other part of the bolts if you can find them."

"I'm not sure where they are, but should they turn up, I will get them to you."

"Well, we'll just have to do the best we can with what we have, won't we."

"I guess we will," I said.

"I take it you are not going to give me any clues to help me?" he said with a grin.

"I would prefer that you tell me everything you can about the items. Then I will tell you where I got the items."

"Okay. The seatbelt harness is typical of those used in sports cars for road racing."

"That item, I would like you to examine to see if it has been tampered with so it would fail to stay together in a crash. As for the bolts, I would like to know what they are from, and what caused the three to break. The odd bolt, I would like to know what kind of a car it is from, and what part of the car used it."

"That's a lot of information. I'll have to have all this for a couple of days."

"That's fine. I should tell you that there are a couple of men who would rather you didn't examine these items too closely."

The professor turned and looked at me. I wasn't sure what he was thinking, but I was pretty sure he got the message.

"Are these involved in a case you are working on?"

"They are."

"It wouldn't happen to have something to do with the crash of a vintage sports car in Chicago where the driver was killed, would it?"

I looked at Monica. She was looking at me.

"Yes. It does. We are trying to figure out if it was an accident or murder," I said then watched him for his reaction.

"I take it you think foul play is involved?"

"That is the question that I would like the answer to. The police seem to think it was an accident."

"But you don't think so?"

"I don't know if it was an accident or not. I'm hoping you can answer that question. I was hired to find out."

"Okay. I'll do what I can to get you an answer. I'll have it for you in a couple of days. I'll also make sure that the items you have left with me are secure."

"Thanks, Professor. You can get ahold of me at this number," I said as I handed him one of my business cards.

"Monica, it was good to see you again. Are you thinking of coming back to work here at the University?"

"Not at this time. I like working with Nick."

"I wish you well, and don't be a stranger. Both of you are always welcome here."

"Thank you," Monica said.

After thanking the professor for taking on the work it would take to answer my questions, Monica and I left his office and returned to our car. We got in then headed for home.

CHAPTER SIX

We arrived home without further incident. There had been no sign of the two men who had followed us. I parked the car in the garage and began taking our luggage out of the car. When I picked up the luggage and turned to head toward the apartment, I noticed Monica was standing at the back of the car and looking toward the stairs to the second floor where our apartment was located. I set the luggage down when she backed up and moved to the inside corner of the garage. I took a moment to look toward the stairs to the second floor.

"What's up? Did you see something?"

"I think I saw the two men who had been following us. I'm sure they don't live in our unit."

"I don't see them. Where did they go?"

"Around the corner of the building toward the stairs."

I stood back in the shadowy corner inside the garage and watched. Monica moved around behind me and was looking over my shoulder.

It was time to make a decision. Do I go see who is there, or do we wait to see if whoever was there comes back? I decided to go check it out. I opened the trunk of my car and got a gun out of the metal lockbox I kept it in. After checking it to make sure it was ready, I looked at Monica.

"Stay here. Don't come until I call you. If you hear shots fired, call the police immediately, but don't come to me. Stay here until the police arrive."

"Okay. Be careful."

I nodded, then ran across the open area toward the stairs that led to the second floor. After looking around the corner and up the stairs, I began to climb the stairs. Moving slowly in the hope of not being surprised. I was the one who wanted to do the surprising. I worked my way to the second floor.

When I reached the second floor, I peeked around the corner. I could see one of the men standing next to the open door of our apartment. He had his hand inside his coat. It was my guess he had his hand on a gun and was ready to use it. I couldn't see the other man. With the door to our apartment open, it was my guess he was inside our apartment.

The man in front of our apartment turned and looked inside. It was obvious that the man inside was saying something to the man at the door, but I couldn't hear him.

"We best get out of here before they show up. I'm sure they will be home at any minute," the man outside said.

Within seconds, the second man came out of the apartment. As soon as he shut the door, he turned toward the stairs. I stepped out in front of them with my gun pointed at the two men.

"Stop right there and put your hands on your head," I ordered.

They didn't move for a few seconds. I watched them carefully. I got the feeling that the one with his hand inside his coat was thinking about trying for it, but I had my gun pointed directly at him and was watching him.

Everything went to hell in a second. The man who had been in the apartment shifted his weight. When he did, the man with his hand inside his coat drew his gun as he quickly moved to one side.

As he moved, I fired. The slug from my gun hit him in the shoulder causing him to spin around as he fell backward at the same time. I quickly swung my gun so it was pointed at the man by the door. Everything had happened so fast that the man next to the door had frozen. He never even reached for his gun.

"Put your hands up and lean against the wall, and spread 'um. I'm sure you know what to do."

He did what I told him to do. I stepped up behind him, stuck my gun in his back, then frisked him for any weapons. I relieved him of a 9mm Glock.

"Nick, Nick, are you okay?" Monica called from near the bottom of the stairs.

"Yes. Did you call the police?"

"Yes."

"I want you to stay down there so you can direct them here. They will need an ambulance."

"Are you hurt?"

"No."

"I'll call them back and tell them."

"When the police arrive, tell them I'm up here with a gun and that I have the two men who broke into our apartment covered."

"Okay."

"You'll never be able to prove we broke into your apartment," the man against the wall said.

"I wouldn't count on that. You're not wearing gloves so your fingerprints will be in the apartment. That's pretty good evidence that you were in my apartment."

That little comment of mine seemed to take the wind out of his sail. There was also the sound of sirens coming toward us, which might have had something to do with it.

"Looks like your ride is almost here," I said.

"I'll be out of jail before they can get the paperwork done," the man said with a hint of humor in his voice.

"I'm not so sure you will want to be released so quickly since you bungled the job."

He turned his head and looked at me over his shoulder. From the expression on his face he wasn't sure what I meant. I didn't bother to explain it to him. I just let him worry about it.

I heard the police car stop in front of the apartment building. Within seconds I heard footsteps at the bottom of the stairs.

"Mr. McCord?"

"Yeah."

"We are coming up. Do you have control of the suspects?"

"I do. You can come up, but remember I'm the one with the gun in my hand."

I could hear the officers coming up the stairs. It seemed to take them awhile to get to the top, but then I'm sure they were just being cautious because they didn't really know what the situation was. As soon as they saw me, they stepped around the corner.

"We can take it from here, Mr. McCord."

"They're all yours," I said.

I stepped back and watched the officers while they handcuffed the two men. They left the one I shot on the floor for the ambulance crew to pick up. He was in pain, but I doubted that my shot was life threating.

"Say, aren't you a Milwaukee Police Detective? I'm Officer Bill Davis. I attended one of your classes on Preserving Evidence at a Crime Scene."

"I remember you, Davis. If I remember correctly, you aced the course."

"Yes, sir."

"It's good to see you again, but I'm a private investigator now."

"What do we have here?" Davis asked.

"We have two men, I do not know their names, but they broke into my apartment. When I tried to hold them for you, the one lying on the floor tried to shoot me. His gun is over there under that bench. Since he couldn't reach it, I didn't move it. This is the gun I took from this one," I said as I handed the officer the 9 mm Glock.

"I'm sorry, but I will need your gun since you shot someone with it. I'm sure you will get it back soon."

"I understand completely. I'll get it back as soon as they run ballistic test on it, and I get cleared because it was a legal shooting."

"Right." Davis said as I handed him my gun.

"You have a permit to carry a gun?"

"Of course."

I reached in my pocket for my wallet. I took my permit out of my wallet and handed it to him. After he made a few notes on his report, he gave it back to me.

"Here comes the ambulance," Davis's partner said.

We stepped out of the way while the ambulance attendants treated the attacker on the floor. Davis' partner stood by to make sure that the one I shot didn't give anyone any trouble. As soon as he was loaded on the stretcher, Davis's partner went with the patient while Davis sat down on the bench with me and began getting my statement.

We had just started when Monica came up the stairs. Davis looked at her then stood up.

"I'm sorry ma'am, but you can't be here right now. This is …."

"It's okay, Davis, she is my wife and partner."

"Sorry, ma'am."

"Honey, we'll have to get a motel room. Our apartment is a crime scene."

"Did you see what happened here, ma'am?" Davis asked.

"Not really. All I saw was two men nosing around our apartment. Nick investigated while I called the police," Monica said.

"I'll need a statement from you as well. Do you mind waiting on the bench over there while I finish up with Nick?"

"Not at all."

Monica glanced at me, then turned and walked down the hall to a bench and sat down.

It wasn't very long before a couple of detectives arrived at the apartment. The lead detective was Lieutenant Gerrie

Baker. We gave her our statements while the other detective looked over the apartment. Then the forensic people showed up. It was beginning to look like it would be a long night.

About three hours later all the evidence from our apartment had been gathered, and the forensic people left. Lieutenant Baker asked us to come in in the morning to sign our statements. As she was about to leave, she stopped and turned toward me.

"You have been some of the easiest people I have had to deal with in a long time. You seem to know what is going on."

"That might be because I was a police officer in Milwaukee for a number of years."

"I thought I should recognize your name. You were a detective on the Milwaukee force."

"That's right."

"I have just one more question before I go."

"What's that?"

"Do you have some idea what those two were looking for?"

"Yes, I do."

"You do?"

Lieutenant Baker seemed surprised.

"Yes. They were looking for a box that contained some bolts and a seatbelt harness, all from an accident that killed a man. We are not sure it was an accident."

"They didn't have it on them, and we didn't see a box in your apartment."

"That's because it isn't here. It is in a lab getting tested to see if the items had been tampered with causing the accident. If they were tampered with, then it was murder."

"I see. Is this something I might get involved in?"

"I would think only to the extent of attempted robbery of this apartment. However, that might change."

"Let me know if I can be of help," she said."

"I will, and thank you."

"By the way, you can have your apartment back now. Forensic is done with it.

"Thanks."

Lieutenant Baker glanced toward Monica and smiled, then left. Monica watched her as she walked down the stairs and disappeared around the corner.

It was time for us to get our luggage and get into our apartment. I got our luggage while Monica waited outside the apartment. As we walked into the apartment, Monica stopped and looked around. From the look on her face, I was sure she was not too happy about all the carbon black that had been used to get fingerprints off almost everything in the living room.

"I'll help you clean up the place in the morning. Right now, I would like to get to bed and get some rest. It's been a very long day," I said.

"I agree."

We emptied our suitcases, then took a quick shower. It didn't take very long before we were in bed. Monica curled up against me. Within a few minutes she was sound asleep. It took me a little while longer.

CHAPTER SEVEN

I woke early, considering the lateness of the hour that we had gotten to bed. Monica was still sleeping. I thought about getting up, but didn't want to wake her.

My thoughts turned to last night. It was apparent I was not the only one who thought Brandon's death was murder. The two thugs had made that very clear. I had no idea who might be involved, or why anyone would want Brandon dead; but it was clear that someone didn't want me to prove it was murder.

The one thing I did have was at least one good suspect. That suspect was Mrs. Barbara Smith, Brandon's wife. Why she wanted him dead was a question I could not answer, but it looked like she might be the one to have the most to gain.

The more I thought about it, Russell Larson could also be considered a suspect. He seemed to want to help by calling me, even helping me examine the car, but was a little reluctant to provide any real information once I began inspecting it. He also questioned me a lot about what I found as I looked over the car. There was also the possibility it may have been not knowing what I was thinking that made him so curious.

Josh could be considered a suspect, too. I was more inclined to think of him as sort of a sub-suspect, but that could change. He worked for Barbara Smith and was probably ready and willing to do almost anything for her. The question that came to mind was he willing to kill for her?

There was always the possibility that there was someone else who I knew nothing about, yet. Possibly someone who didn't like Brandon for some reason that was still unknown to me.

I knew that all this was speculation on my part. I only had a few things to go on, and none of them were very good at this time. Background checks, financial records, and criminal reports on those I thought might be involved was something that might help reduce my list of suspects. However, experience had taught me that it was more likely to add to it.

I knew just the man to get me their criminal records and arrest reports. An old friend that worked as a Desk Sergeant at Second Precinct in the Milwaukee Police Department. He would be able to get criminal reports on all my suspects.

Monica and I could get the financial reports, credit checks, and background checks on each and every suspect on our computers.

Just then, Monica rolled over and looked at me. I smiled at her.

"What have you been thinking about?" Monica asked.

"I was running a short list of people through my head who, I think, might be suspects in Brandon's death."

"So, you think it was murder?"

"I have no doubt that it was murder. The only questions are why and who?"

"That should make it easy," she laughed.

"Very funny."

"I think it is time to get some breakfast, then go to the police station and sign our statements."

"You're right."

I leaned over and kissed Monica, then sat up.

"I'll take a quick shower then start breakfast."

"Okay," she replied.

I got up, took a shower, and dressed, then went into the kitchen. As I passed through the living room, I noticed the carbon black that had been left behind by the forensic crew while dusting for fingerprints. It was a stark reminder of what had happened here last evening.

It also reminded me that we have an apartment to clean up. That thought caused me to think it might be a good idea to take our time in cleaning up the place. There was no telling what we might find that the police missed. That would have to wait until later.

Once in the kitchen, I began preparing breakfast. It wasn't long before Monica showed up. It was obvious that she had just stepped out of the shower. She was wearing a robe that accented her figure very nicely.

"Other than going to the police station, what else did you have in mind for today?" she asked.

"I figured after we sign our statements, we would come back here and clean up the place. Breakfast is ready."

"In that case, we'll eat then I'll get ready to go."

We sat down and had breakfast. Neither of us talked much. I guess our minds were on what happened here last evening. Once we were finished, I cleaned up the kitchen while Monica got dressed.

As soon as we were ready, we left for the police station to sign our statements.

When we arrived at the police station, the Desk Sergeant pointed to a hallway and told us Lieutenant Gerrie Baker's office was "down that way". It didn't take us long to find Lieutenant Baker's office. I knocked on the door and we were quickly told to enter. We stepped into the office and found Lieutenant Baker sitting at her desk. She immediately stood up.

"Please come in. Have a seat," she said as she pointed to the chairs in front of her desk.

"Thank you," Monica said.

"I hope you got a good night's sleep."

"We slept pretty good, considering," I said.

"I'm sure. I have both of your statements here. Would you please read them and sign them if they are correct?"

She handed Monica her statement first, then handed me mine. I read over the statement. It appeared to be correct as to what I said last evening. I couldn't be one hundred percent sure it was my exact words, but it was close enough that the meaning of what I said was clear. I signed the statement and handed it back to Lieutenant Baker.

I glanced over at Monica. She seemed to have some difficulty with her statement.

"What's the problem, Honey."

"I'm not sure this is what I said."

"I know it is hard to remember what you said word for word, but does it have the meaning of what you said, and is it very close to the words you used?"

"Yes. It does express the meaning of what I said even if it might not be the actual words I used."

"Is there something in it you would like to change?" Lieutenant Baker asked.

"No, not really. It is clearly what I meant. It's just that I'm not sure I used those words."

"It isn't often that we use the same words to say the same thing twice, especially after a few hours go by. Let me put it this way, does the statement express what you said, and what you said clearly?" Lieutenant Baker asked.

"Yes. It does do that," Monica said.

"Then that is what we want."

Monica looked at her for a moment, then at me. I could see that she was thinking about what had been said. She then signed the statement and handed it back to Lieutenant Baker.

"Thank you."

"What happened to the two men you arrested last evening?" I asked.

"The one you shot is still in the hospital under arrest. I might add he has been screaming that you shot him without reason. We have him for carrying a concealed weapon without a permit, attempted robbery and attempted murder."

"It doesn't surprise me that he is screaming his head off. He's looking at some serious jail time. What about the other one?"

"He was arrested and put in jail. His attorney got him out on bail this morning. He claimed that he never shot or drew his weapon, he went peacefully when you held him for the police. He claimed that he broke into your apartment, but he didn't steal anything."

"I take it he was charged with breaking and entering, and that was it."

"That is correct."

"Did he have a permit to carry a concealed weapon?"

"As a matter of fact, yes, he did."

"By the way, who was his attorney?"

"Some guy from Chicago," Lieutenant Baker said as she opened a file in front of her on the desk. "His name is . . ."

"Let me guess. His name was George Moorhouse."

"Yeah. How is it you know that?"

"I met him at Barbara Smith's home in Calumet City, Illinois."

"Would you be kind enough to explain that?"

"I'm investigating the death of Brandon Smith. He died in the car crash of his vintage Ferrari at a racetrack near Chicago after the car show in Chicago."

"Read something about that in the paper. If I remember correctly, the Chicago Police said it was an accident."

"It may have been an accident, but I don't think so. I have a few parts from the car being analyzed at the University of Wisconsin's Engineering Department to see if they had been tampered with and caused the car to crash."

"The two thugs that broke into your apartment were there to find the parts in order to prevent you from having them examined. Is that correct?" Baker asked.

"You grasp the situation very quickly," I said.

"This was more than a simple robbery, then."

"That is correct."

"How can I help you?"

"At this point, I don't think there is much you can do other than maybe have a patrol car hanging around the area so they can respond quickly if we should have to call for help again," I suggested.

"I can keep a patrol car in the area for a little while, maybe for a week to ten days."

"That would be fine, and we appreciate your help."

"Give me a call if I can be of any further help."

"I will, and thank you."

"You understand that I am limited by jurisdiction?"

"Yes, I understand that."

Monica and I stood up and walked toward the door. Just as we got to the door, Lieutenant Baker spoke.

"Good luck."

"I'll probably need a little luck," I said.

I smiled at her then turned and left her office. We walked out of the police station toward my car. As I opened the door for Monica, I glanced over the top of the car. There was a blue Dodge parked across the street with a man sitting in it. I couldn't see the man very well, but the car looked familiar.

I walked around to the other side of the car and got in. Monica looked at me as if she was concerned about something.

"I noticed you looking at the blue car across the street. Is there a problem?"

"I'm not sure. We'll have to keep an eye on it."

I reached down, turned the key and started the car. After backing out of the parking space, I drove to the exit of the parking lot. When it was clear of traffic, I turned out onto the street and headed toward downtown.

The blue sedan was facing the opposite direction from the way I turned onto the street. I looked in the rearview mirror. The blue sedan was making a U turn and would soon be following us.

"I think we have a tail."

"The blue sedan?"

"Yes. Call Lieutenant Baker and ask her if she has someone following us."

"You think she might have someone following us?"

"No, but she might, just to make sure we are safe. I want to make sure it's not one of her people before I decide to shake them off our tail."

I kept an eye on the blue sedan behind us while Monica called Lieutenant Baker. She put her cell phone on speaker.

"Sergeant Wilson, is this an emergency?"

"No. I would like to talk to Lieutenant Baker, please."

"Your name, please."

"Monica McCord."

"One moment."

It didn't take but a second or two before Lieutenant Baker came on the phone.

"Hi, Monica. Did you forget something?"

"No. Nick would like to know if you put a tail on us. We have a blue sedan following us. It picked us up just outside the police station."

"No. I didn't put a tail on you. Why would I do that?"

"Lieutenant, this is Nick. You seemed concerned for us so I thought we should check with you first. I'll try to get a license plate number for you."

"I can have a unit catch up to you if you let me know where you are."

"I don't think that will be necessary. As soon as I get a plate number, I'll ditch him."

"I'll stay on the line," she said.

We were coming up on a traffic light and it was changing to red. It forced the blue sedan to pull up behind me. As it did, I was able to get a plate number.

Monica told Lieutenant Baker the plate number, and reported that there was only one person in the car that we could see. We were unable to identify the person in the car because of the glare on the windshield.

"I'll run the number for you. Give me a moment."

As the light turned green, I pulled away from the intersection. Several cars had pulled up in the lane on my right while we were at the stoplight. As soon as the light changed, I quickly pulled ahead of the cars and moved over in front of them and slowed down enough to force the blue sedan to stay in the left lane, unless he planned to pass us. When we came to a corner, I turned right onto another street and sped down to the next corner. I made another right turn and then another. It soon put us back on the street we had been on. We continued on toward our apartment.

Suddenly a voice came over Monica's cell phone.

"You still there?" Lieutenant Baker asked.

"Yes," Monica replied.

"The license plate number is registered to a rental company. It's Any Time Rentals. They rent all sorts of things including cars. It's a locally owned business, not one of the national car rental companies."

"Any idea who owns the business?" I asked.

"No, but I'll see if I can find out for you. I'll call you back."

"Thanks," I said then had Monica hang up.

"Where to now?" Monica asked.

"I think we'll go home and clean up the place."

Monica looked at me for a moment, then looked out the windshield. I noticed that she glanced at the outside rearview mirror from time to time. I guess I couldn't blame her. I also kept an eye out for someone following us.

It didn't take us very long to get to our apartment. We both kept an eye out as I parked the car and walked up to our apartment.

Just as we got inside the apartment, Monica's cell phone began to ring. Monica answered it as she sat down on the sofa. I sat down beside her.

"Hello."

"Monica, this is Lieutenant Baker. I found out that the place the blue car was rented from is owned by a company in Chicago. The company is owned by a William F. Stoker. Does the name ring any bells with either of you?"

"Lieutenant, this is Nick. I've heard that name somewhere before. If I recall, William F. Stoker is rather rich and owns several vintage automobiles. Now I remember where I saw that name. It was in the Chicago newspaper. He showed several cars at the Concours De'Alligance Show in Chicago, the same show where Brandon Smith showed his vintage 1954 Ferrari roadster."

"Do you think there's a connection?"

"I don't know, but it sure wouldn't hurt to dig into it."

"You be careful around him. He's got a lot of influential friends, including judges and attorneys."

"And one of those attorneys wouldn't happen to be George Moorhouse, would it?"

"It could be. I have a friend on the Chicago force who might know. I'll give him a call," Lieutenant Baker said."

"Thanks, and thanks for your help."

"I'll get back to you," Lieutenant Baker said then hung up.

Monica just sat there looking at me. I had a pretty good idea what was going through her mind. I was thinking the same thing. I was thinking that we might have another suspect, that being William F. Stoker.

"What do we do now?" Monica asked.

"We clean up this place while we wait to hear back from Baker. It could take her a while."

Monica smiled, then stood up. We gathered what we would need to clean up the mess made by the forensic team, then went to work.

CHAPTER EIGHT

We had just finished cleaning the apartment and sat down for a cup of coffee when Monica's cell phone began to ring. Monica looked at me and smiled as she got up. She walked to where she had left her phone and answered it.

"Hello."

"Monica, this is Lieutenant Baker. I have the information Nick requested."

"Hi, this is Nick. I can hear you."

"I talked to my friend on the Chicago force. He told me that Stoker is pretty well known by the Chicago Police force, and not in a likeable way."

"I take it they have had their problems with him."

"That's putting it mildly. Several of the Chicago detectives who have had run-ins with him think he is as crooked as a cow's hind leg, but have been unable to prove it."

"Is George Moorhouse his attorney?"

"Yes, but just one of them. From what I was able to gather, Moorhouse is the one who handles most, if not all, of the criminal charges lodged against Stoker and his cronies. He also has several lawyers who handle his business dealings.

"I might add that there have been plenty of criminal charges, but none of them have been proven. He hasn't spent a single night in jail."

"I was told that Moorhouse was Barbara Smith's business attorney. It seems he is much more than a criminal attorney, if he is her business attorney."

"Is Mrs. Smith your client?"

"You could say that. She hired us to find out if Brandon Smith, her husband, was murdered, or if his death was an accident as the Chicago Police have stated after their inspection of his car at the racetrack."

"That seems strange," Lieutenant Baker said.

"Yes, it is. This whole thing is strange. We now have a connection between Stoker, Mrs. Smith and Moorhouse. Granted, it's pretty thin, but it can't be overlooked."

"I agree. I have to go. Let me know if there is anything else I can do for you."

"Thanks, Lieutenant," I said then hung up.

I looked at Monica. She was looking at me. She seemed as confused as I was, and I didn't like what I was thinking. It was beginning to look like things were getting even more complicated.

I also got the feeling that I was being played for a sucker by Mrs. Smith, and I don't like it one bit. She just might find that I will point a finger at her as quickly as I would at anyone who I find has committed a crime.

"What do we do now," Monica asked.

"I'm not sure. I think the next thing we need to do is check in with Professor Houzerman. I'd like to know what he found out about the evidence we left with him."

"When do we do that?"

"Right now."

We got up and headed for the door. Just as I was about to open the door, the phone in our office began to ring. I looked at Monica. She shrugged her shoulders. I turned and went into our office, and picked up the phone.

"McCord Detective Agency, how may I help you?"

"Is this Nick McCord?" a whispery voice said.

"Yes. Who is this?"

"You don't know me, but I might have somethin' that you would like to have."

"You'll have to tell me more, like what your name is."

"I'm one of the track workers at the racetrack near Chicago where that driver was killed in his fancy old Ferrari. I found somethin' that you might be interested in."

"What did you find that you think I might be interested in?"

"What's it worth to you to have what I found?"

"That would depend on two things, where you got it and what it is. I'm sure not going to buy something without knowing what it is, and how important it is to me."

There was dead silence on the phone. I could hear something in the background, but I couldn't make out what it was. It was possible that this guy found something that might be important to my investigation, and it would be best to hear him out.

After waiting for a minute or so for him to decide if he was going to tell me, I decided to put him on the spot.

"If you found something that is important to finding out what caused the crash of Brandon's vintage Ferrari, and you don't give it to the police, you could end up in a lot of trouble for withholding evidence."

"I'm afraid to give it to the police. I liked Mr. Smith. He was always nice to me."

"Why are you afraid to give it to the police?"

"I'm an ex-con. If I give it to them, it just might get lost. They would say I was just looking to make them look bad, 'cause they didn't find it where the car crashed."

"Okay. Tell me what you found and where you found it. I will tell you if it might be important to my investigation," I said thinking he just might have something important.

"I wouldn't get into trouble if I give it to you, will I?"

"No. You will not get into trouble if you give it to me because I won't tell anyone where I got it. However, you might get into a lot of trouble if you don't give it to me."

"Okay," he said followed by a long pause. "I was on cleanup crew on the racetrack, ya see. After Mr. Smith's car was hauled off to the garage where the police looked at it, I was sweeping up the track where the crash happened, I found something that I didn't think should have been there."

"What was it you found?"

"I found a piece of metal and the ends of three bolts. The three bolts still had the nuts on 'um. They was just lyin' at the edge of the guardrail, ya know, next to the guardrail where the car hit it."

This guy might have found something important, if they were the missing ends of the bolts I had already given to Professor Houzerman.

"What did you do with what you found?"

"Well, I picked 'um up and put 'um in my pocket of my coveralls. I was goin' to put 'um in with some other scrap metal, but by the time I got back to the maintenance shop, I sorta forgot all about 'um, ya know," he said, then stopped.

"Go on," I said.

"Well, I hung up my coveralls after work that evenin' and didn't think about 'um until I returned to work, yesterday. When I put my coveralls on, I felt 'um in my pocket. They was still there. I had heard that there was some question about the accident that Mr. Smith might have been murdered, and that you was lookin' to see if the car had been messed with."

"How did you know to call me?"

"I overheard one of the cleanup crew guys tell someone that you was the one Mr. Larson called to look into the accident, and that he, that's Mr. Larson, thought it might have been murder. I got to thinkin' that those pieces of bolts might have somethin' to do with it, ya know. So after I gave it some thought, I called ya."

"That was good thinking on your part. What's your name?"

He hesitated for a minute or so. I wasn't sure he was going to tell me his name.

"Billy Ricker. You won't tell anyone I called ya, will ya?"

"No. I won't say a word. I'd like to see you and get the piece of metal you mentioned as well as the bolts. I don't know what value they are to my investigation, but they could be important, very important. Would it be all right if I come and get what you found?"

Again, there was silence on the phone.

"I guess it would be okay, but I'd rather ya don't see me at work. Someone might see ya talkin' to me. I don't know who I can trust around here no more."

"Okay, Billy. Where would you like me to meet you?"

"Not at the racetrack. I'll put the things I found in my lunch box and take 'um home. Maybe ya could come to my house in the evenin' and pick 'um up."

"Okay. I can do that. Would this evening be okay with you?" I asked.

"I guess so. Yeah, sure. It would be best if you come after seven this evenin'."

Billy told me where the racetrack was located and where he lived. The racetrack where the vintage cars had raced was actually located in one of the suburbs of Chicago. Billy lived about fifteen miles from the racetrack, which actually made it a little closer for me.

After getting the information and directions to where he lived, I thanked him and told him I would be there by about eight o'clock in the evening. He agreed that it would be a good time to come, and that he would have the piece of metal and the three partial bolts at his house to give to me.

With everything arranged, I hung up. As I turned around to talk to Monica, I saw her standing in the doorway smiling.

"You heard?"

"I did. It sounds like we are going for a drive this evening."

"That would be correct, but not before I look up some information on the racetrack. I thought we could leave about two-thirty this afternoon and grab something to eat before we go see him."

"Why so early, if we are not meeting him until eight o'clock?" Monica asked.

"I want to get there early so we can check out the area. I would like to know if his home is being watched. I would also like to drive by the private racetrack. It might prove interesting to know who owns it."

"That's probably a good idea. It's a little past noon. How about something to eat now?"

"Good idea."

We fixed sandwiches then sat down to eat lunch. We didn't talk much, probably because we had a lot on our minds.

I couldn't help but think that Ricker might be in danger if the wrong person found out that he had the three ends of the bolts and the piece of metal. He seemed like he was being careful. I just hoped he was being careful enough.

Just thinking about the bolts and piece of metal got me to thinking that this could prove that Brandon was murdered. Then again, what Ricker found might not have anything to do with the crash of Brandon's Ferrari.

I had just finished my sandwich when the phone began to ring, again. I went into the office and answered the phone.

"McCord Detective Agency, how may I help you?"

"Nick, this is Professor Houzerman."

"It's good to hear from you. I hope you have good news for me."

"I don't know if it is good news or not. I tested the partial bolts you left with me. It seems that the bolts are from a Ferrari, but were not of the same material makeup of the ones that should have been used to hold the suspension system to the frame."

"What? What do you mean?" I asked.

"They were not the right bolts for what they had been used for. They didn't have the strength they should have had to be used to hold the suspension system to the frame."

"Let me see if I understand you correctly. Your telling me that the bolts that were used to connect the suspension system to the car were the wrong bolts and not strong enough for the suspension system?"

"That is correct. The bolts you gave me were not designed for stresses they would have been put to if used on the suspension system, especially if the car was raced and the suspension was put under a lot of stress," Professor Houzerman said.

"What about the complete nut and bolt that was found?"

"That was actually the correct bolt. In other words, that is the kind of bolt that should have been used to connect the suspension system to the frame. But there should have been three bolts just like it holding the suspension."

"What do you think happened?" I asked.

"It would be my guess that the three bolts could not take the stress they were put to during the race and simply broke. That caused the suspension to break away from the frame which caused the driver to lose control of the car resulting in the crash that caused the driver's death."

"I will need to contact Larson, Brandon's mechanic, and find out who worked on the car's suspension system."

"I'm afraid that this doesn't help you determine if it was an accident because someone used the wrong bolts, or if the bolts were changed in an effort to kill the driver, at the very least, destroy the car. This could have been a simple accident caused by someone's carelessness by not using the right bolts."

"You're right about that. It really causes more questions than it answers."

"I would think so. I'm sorry I couldn't be more help."

"Thanks for your help. You have been a big help. I will need a written report on your findings."

"No problem. I'll get it written up and call you when it's ready.

"Send me the bill for your work when you're done," I said.

"I will," the professor said, then hung up.

I hung up the phone and looked at Monica standing in the doorway.

"What did the professor have to say?" Monica asked.

"The bolts were the wrong bolts for where they were used."

"Wouldn't that indicate that someone tampered with the car?"

"It certainly would."

"If the bolts used were not the right ones, wouldn't that eliminate Larson as a suspect. He certainly would know what bolts to use."

"Not really."

"Why?"

"Larson may have replaced the right bolts with the ones that wouldn't be able to stand the stress from the car during a race. Not a lot of people know one bolt from another, or how to tell if it was the right bolt. Bolts are made from different materials of different strengths. Most specialty bolts, like those used on Ferraris, are coded with a stamped number on the head of the bolt. The three partial bolts we took to the professor didn't have any markings on the bolt heads, as I recall."

"What about the bolt with the nut still on it?"

"According to the professor, that was the kind of bolt that should have been used. We had one, but there should have been a total of four bolts."

"Maybe that bolt was on the suspension, but got dropped when it was changed for the weaker bolts. The person changing the bolts either didn't realize it had been dropped, or he couldn't find it in his hurry to get away from the car."

"That makes for a good scenario on what might have happened. It would explain why the bolt that should have been used was lying on the trailer bed."

"What do we do now?" Monica asked.

"I'll look up the information on the racetrack, then we'll go to visit Mr. Ricker."

I turned to my computer while Monica left the office. I looked up the racetrack that was used for the vintage car race. It didn't take long before I was able to get a lot of information, including who used it and the names of organizations that rented it.

The racetrack belonged to an individual who used it to show off cars, teach wannabe race car drivers, and rented the track to different organizations who wanted to use it for fund raising. There were also some amateur sports car races on weekends during the summer.

While looking through information on who had rented the track recently, I noted that it had been rented by the Chicago Antique Car Club which was one of the major sponsors of the car show and the only sponsor of the vintage car race. I noted that one of the officers of the Antique Car Club was none other than William F. Stoker. It also listed several of the people who were involved in putting on the race. They included Mrs. Barbara Smith and George Moorhouse, along with several other prominent names in the Chicago area.

I now had the information I needed. It was time to pay a visit to the racetrack.

Monica and I got ready to leave the apartment. Before I left the apartment, I took a minute to look out the window over the parking lot. I was looking to see if anyone might be watching the apartment. I wasn't disappointed. Off on the other side of a row of parked cars was a blue sedan. It looked like the one I had ditched earlier.

I went into the office and got my binoculars out of the closet for a closer look. After returning to the window, I checked out the blue sedan. I could not read all of the license plate, but I could read enough of it to know that it was the same car.

I turned around and saw Monica watching me. She looked at the binoculars, then looked at me.

"We have a problem, don't we?"

"Only a small one."

"The blue sedan?"

"Yes. I sort of expected it. When we ditched him, he had no choice but to come here if he wanted to pick us up again."

"What now?"

"A call to Lieutenant Baker should take care of the problem."

I walked over to the phone and called Lieutenant Baker. It didn't take but a minute or so before she was on the phone.

"Good afternoon, Nick. What's up?"

"I could use a black and white unit to roll into the parking lot where my apartment building is located. I got a guy watching me and I don't want to be followed. I would like the unit to delay him for a few minutes while I leave."

"Is it someone who might be of interest to the police?"

"I would think so, but I'm not a hundred percent sure. All I want the officers to do is to question him as to why he is parked in the parking lot. I'm sure they can delay him for a good ten or fifteen minutes just checking his driver's license and questioning him about why he is parked there since he doesn't live in this apartment complex."

"I can do that. I'll have a unit sent out there immediately."

"Thanks. It's a blue sedan."

I gave her the license plate number then hung up.

"Now we wait. As soon as the police have stopped by the blue sedan, we leave. Be ready. I'll watch for the police."

It didn't take long for the black and white unit to arrive. As soon as the police had the blue sedan pinned in the parking space and were getting out of their unit, we left the apartment. The officers were talking to the driver as we drove out of the parking lot. I only hoped they would keep the driver busy long enough for us to get out of the area.

CHAPTER NINE

We were well on our way to meet Ricker at his home, but I wanted to visit the racetrack before we talked to Ricker. I kept an eye out for the blue sedan, but didn't see it again.

It took us about two and a half hours to get to the private racetrack where Brandon had crashed his vintage Ferrari. I pulled up in front of the main gate, but didn't see anyone. It almost looked as if the place was deserted. I tooted the horn and waited. It only took about a minute or so before a man in coveralls came out of the garage near the gate. He stepped through a small gate and walked up to our car.

"Sorry, mister, we are not open today."

"My name in Nick McCord. I'm investigating the crash of Brandon Smith's vintage Ferrari here."

He looked at me suspiciously before he said anything.

"I can tell you this much, the crash of that car had nothing to do with the racetrack."

"I'm sure you are right. May I ask who you are?

"I'm the owner of this track. The state has had people out here looking at the track to see if it might have caused the crash. They told me there was nothing about the track that would have caused the car to crash, or even played a part in the accident or the death of the driver."

"I'm not here to judge the condition of your racetrack. I just want to see where the crash took place, and ask you a few questions."

Again, he just stood there looking at me.

"Okay. I'm Jesse Williams. I'll open the gate so you can drive in."

"Thank you."

As soon as he had the gate open, he pointed to a place where I should park. I parked the car and got out. Monica got out and walked around the car where she joined me.

"What questions do you have of me? I already talked to the police who investigated the accident, and the state racing officials who examined the track. The police said it was an accident and the state officials cleared the track of having any part in causing the accident, or contributing to the accident."

"I'm sure you are right. I'd like to walk out to where the accident happened."

"Say, are you a newspaper man?"

"No, I'm a private investigator," I said.

I reached in my pocket and got out my Private Investigator license and badge to show him. He looked at it for a moment before he looked back at me.

"Apparently whoever hired you thinks it wasn't an accident."

"That would be correct. Can we go out to where the accident happened?"

"Yeah. I don't have anything to hide. It's a hike to walk out there. Let's take the golf cart over there."

Monica and I got in the golf cart. Mr. Williams drove. We rode around the track in the golf cart until we were where the accident happened. It was at the back of the track.

It was clear that we were where the 'accident' had happened. I could see the place where the guardrail had been damaged. There was red paint on the damaged area of the guardrail. It looked like Ferrari red, which made sense. We got out of the golf cart and walked over to the guardrail.

"This is where the car hit the guardrail," Mr. Williams said. "I will be replacing that section of the guardrail next week. I had to wait for the state to examine it before I could replace it."

"I understand. Did you see the accident?"

"Yes."

"Where were you at that time?"

"I was in the tower just above the main grandstands. I can see the entire track from up there, with exception of about a hundred yards of the fourth turn. View of the cars is partially blocked where the track goes down behind a slight hill for a short way. It then comes back up to the highest point on the track just before the fifth turn. The fourth turn is also the farthest turn from the grandstands, and the only place where the cars cannot be seen by anyone in the grandstands."

"How long would you estimate the cars are out of sight at the fourth turn?"

"Oh, depending on how fast they are going, I would say, - - about three to four seconds on average."

"Would that be a good estimate for the vintage race cars?"

"Well, they don't push the cars as hard as the newer cars. It's very expensive to fix them when they get damaged. Also, many of the drivers are not skilled race car drivers, so they're a little more careful. I would say a good estimate for a vintage race car driven by a non-professional driver might by five to six seconds, maybe as long as seven seconds. It might be slightly more for the first-time drivers on this track."

"I understand Brandon had lessons before he drove here. Is that something you know anything about?"

"He showed me a certificate for a race car driver course he completed in California some time ago. I believe it was at Riverside Raceway. That racetrack is no longer there. I do know that he was a good driver, and he had raced on this track before."

"How many times had he raced here?"

"About five or six times, I would guess. I can look it up, if you want."

"I don't think that will be necessary. So, he knew the course pretty well?"

"I would say so. Sure."

"I'd like to walk back to the fourth turn and start there. I want to walk the track from there to just past the fifth turn."

"Fine with me. I'll help you look if you can tell me what you are looking for."

"Something that doesn't belong here, or something unusual."

"Okay," he said.

Jesse walked alongside me as I walked back to the fourth corner. It was my guess that something happened at that corner which started a chain reaction that caused stress on the front suspension causing it to fail and crash into the guardrail in the fifth corner. I wanted to know what it was, even though finding anything helpful was a long shot at best.

Knowing that a race car driven by an experienced race car driver tends to run low on the apex of the corner, I started where the corner began. I didn't see anything at the beginning of the turn. It was when I was about halfway through the corner that I noticed a place where the pavement had a gouge in it. It was only about six or seven inches long, and maybe an inch to an inch and a half wide at the widest point, but only a half inch deep at the deepest spot.

I knelt down to take a closer look at it. It looked like the gouge in the pavement was from something that had hit the pavement at a very high speed. A closer look at it, showed me that whatever made the gouge in the pavement came from the direction toward the normal flow of cars on the track.

"Did you find something?" Jesse asked.

"I'm not sure. Was there any kind of an accident here on this corner, say within a few days before the race, or even during the race?"

"No. We didn't have anyone on the track since the weekend before the race that killed Mr. Smith."

"Can you tell me what might have made this gouge in the pavement?"

I watched as Jesse knelt down and looked at it. He turned his head and looked up at me."

"Have no idea what made it. I'm sure it wasn't there before the race. I always walk the track before I open the track for racing. I like to make sure the track is in good condition and clear of any debris."

"What position was Brandon in when he had the accident?"

"He was leading."

"So, all the other cars were behind him. He was the first one through the corner?"

"Yes. He was on his twenty-eighth lap, I believe."

"How many laps were they running in that race?"

"Just thirty-two."

"Was anyone close to him?"

"Not that I recall. I think he was leading the next car by maybe five or six car lengths, maybe a little more."

I looked back at the corner. If he was five or six car lengths ahead of the car behind him, Brandon would have been in the corner all by himself.

"So, Brandon would have been out of corner four before the next car entered corner four, is that correct?"

"That would be correct. What are you getting at?"

"One more question. Did Brandon possibly blow a tire as he came out of corner four?"

"Yes. I think you're right. He blew the tire just as he was coming out of corner four. It was the left front tire. That was probably what caused the accident."

"I'm sure that the tire came apart when it blew?"

"Yes, it did. There were parts of the tire all over the track."

"I know you have a crew that cleans up the track after a race or an accident."

"That's right."

"Where do they put what they sweep up?" I asked.

"We put things like that in a dumpster on the back of a truck. When it gets full, we take it to the dump. Why?"

"Has it been taken to the dump since the race?"

"No, I don't think so. The last time I looked at it, it wasn't even half full. I take it you want to look through what is in it."

"Yes."

"What do you hope to find?"

"I believe the gouge in the pavement was made by a bullet. I think someone shot the tire causing it to blow. I'm hoping that we might find a piece of the tire that has a bullet hole in it."

"Good luck with that," Jesse said. "When a tire blows, it would come apart in a lot of small pieces at the speed Mr. Smith was going. It would be next to impossible to find a small bullet hole in any of the pieces."

"I know it's a long shot at best. But not to at least look at the pieces of tire would be to not check out for all possible evidence. Don't you agree?"

"I guess so. I have some coveralls you can use while you look. No need to get your clothes dirty climbing around inside the dumpster."

"I'll get to that after I've looked over turn five where he hit the guardrail."

I walked on down the track looking for anything that might be of interest. When I reached the place where the car had crashed against the guardrail, I didn't find anything I didn't expect to find. The track crew did a good job of cleaning up the track.

I did take a few minutes to climb over the guardrail and walk back toward turn four. I found a place where it would be an easy shot at a car coming around turn four, but didn't find anything to indicate there might have been someone there. I didn't find any shell casing, any footprints, or anything else that would prove there had been someone there. The only hint that someone might have been there was some weeds that looked like they had been stepped on, but there was no way to know when it happened or who or what might have stepped on the weeds.

When I finished my inspection of the track, we returned to the office. Jesse took me around back to the truck with the dumpster on it. I quickly found that it was empty. I looked at Jesse.

"One of the cleanup crew must have taken it to the dump," Jesse said.

I wasn't sure if it was done to get rid of evidence, or if it was simply full and needed to go to the dump. Either way, it was gone and highly unlikely that it would have any evidence in it. If there had been, it was probably destroyed by now.

"I guess I won't need the coveralls." I said.

"I'm sorry. I didn't know that the grounds crew had taken it to the dump."

"It's okay. It was a long shot at best, anyway. Thank you for your cooperation."

"If there is anything else I can do, please let me know. I don't really want any black marks on my racetrack," Jesse said.

"I understand. We'll be leaving."

I shook his hand, then Monica and I returned to our car. Once in the car, I sat there for a minute thinking and just looking out the car windshield.

"Where to now?" Monica asked.

Monica's comment shook me from my thoughts.

"I think we should go see Ricker," I said as I started the car.

We left the racetrack and headed for the address that Ricker had given me over the phone. I glanced at Monica and could tell she wanted to say something.

"What's on your mind, Honey."

"What were you thinking about back there?"

"Based on what I saw at the track, I get the feeling that someone may have helped the accident along by shooting out one of the tires.

"How would that help?" Monica asked.

"By shooting out a tire, the car would quickly become unstable. It would cause Brandon to make hard and fast corrections in the car in an effort to keep it from crashing. That action would put a lot of extra stress on the front suspension."

"And that would cause the weaker bolts to break, causing the car to crash," she added.

"That's right. There were only four laps left before the race would end. Maybe, whoever wanted Brandon out of the race was getting impatient since the front suspension hadn't broken, and decided it needed a little help."

"It couldn't have been anyone who was driving in the race," Monica said.

"That's true, but it could be someone who worked for, or was hired by, someone in the race."

"That doesn't put us any closer to who had caused the crash."

"No, it doesn't. I think it might be a good idea if we get a list of those in the race. It might help us find someone who would have a good reason to kill Brandon. It would have to be someone who could afford to hire a pretty good marksman. The average shooter would have a hard time shooting and hitting the tire of a car moving at that speed. There is a very good chance that the shooter missed the tire and all he did was put a grove in the pavement of the track."

"Don't think there are any of the people that showed cars like those we have been talking about who couldn't afford a shooter, Monica."

"You're probably right about that," I said.

On the way to Ricker's home, we stopped at a restaurant for dinner. The food was good, but I was more interested in what happened at the racetrack. Monica and I talked for a while about the vintage cars and about Mrs. Smith. We both felt that she was using us, but we agreed that we would do all we could to find who had murdered Brandon even if it took us right to the front door of Mrs. Smith's estate.

CHAPTER TEN

After leaving the restaurant, we headed to Ricker's home. We didn't talk much. I think we were both deep in our own thoughts about who might have wanted to kill Brandon. I know I could think of several people who might want him dead, but connecting them to the so called 'accident' was going to be very difficult.

It had taken us about twenty-five minutes to get to the street that Ricker's home was located on. When we found Ricker's house, I pulled up in front of the house and stopped. We sat in the car and looked at the house for a minute.

It was a small house in a small housing development where most of the houses looked almost alike, and probably had almost the same floor plans. From the looks of the houses, they had been built in the late fifties or early sixties.

There was a single car garage at the end of a fairly long driveway. The garage was toward the back of the house. The garage door was closed so I could not tell if there was a vehicle in the garage.

The outside of the house looked like it had been well maintained over the years. The lawn was neatly mowed and trimmed. I didn't see any flowers, but the few shrubs around the front of the house were also nicely trimmed. We could not see any lights on in the house that could be seen from the street.

"It doesn't look like anyone's home," Monica said.

"It's still light enough that he might not have turned on any lights upstairs. I noticed there was a light in one of the basement windows when we pulled up. Maybe he's working on something in the basement. Let's go knock on the door."

I got out of the car and walked around it. I opened the door and gave Monica a hand. We walked up to the door and rang the doorbell. I could hear it ring. There was no answer. I rang it again, but still no answer. A quick look at my wrist watch showed me that it was a few minutes past eight o'clock, the hour we agreed to meet.

I began to worry that something might have happened to him, or he had decided that he didn't want to talk to me. I was hoping that this trip to see him wasn't a waste of time.

"Do you think he might have decided he didn't want to get involved?" Monica asked.

"I had that same thought. I think I'll walk around to the garage and see if his car is there."

I left Monica at the front door in case Ricker came to the door, then walked around to the side of the house and started along the drive toward the garage. As I walked by one of the basement windows, I could see there was a light on. I took a second to bend down to look in the basement window.

As I looked in, it stopped me up short. There on the floor of the basement was the body of a man. He was wearing work clothes, dark blue pants and matching shirt with the logo of the private racetrack where Ricker worked. I could see blood on the floor, a lot of it, around the area of his head. I could also see the face of the victim. His eyes were not completely shut indicating to me that he was probably dead. With the amount of blood on the floor around his head, there was little chance that he was still alive. If I had to guess, it was Ricker's body I was looking at. Since it was his house and the clothes on the body were from where Ricker worked, I still couldn't be one hundred percent positive it was Ricker since I had never seen him.

It was obvious that there was nothing I could do for him. I quickly returned to the front porch.

"I think I found Ricker. He's on the floor in the basement. I need your phone."

The look on Monica's face as she handed me her phone showed me that she had a pretty good idea what had happened to Ricker. I called 9-1-1.

As soon as it was answered, I gave the operator my name, location, and told her what I had found. I told her that

I had not tried to go into the house because it looked like the person on the floor was probably dead. She told me not to try to enter the home, but to stay on the phone until the police arrived.

I did as she instructed. I didn't think it would make any difference to Ricker if I broke into his house or not since he was already dead. However, it might make a difference to the police.

It wasn't but a couple of minutes before I heard the sound of a siren. It was only a couple minutes more before a police car pulled up in front of the house, and two police officers got out of the patrol car.

"The police are here," I told the 9-1-1 operator.

"Please do not leave until they have had a chance to talk to you," she said.

"I will not leave," I said then hung up.

I gave Monica her phone, then waited for the police sergeant to come to me. He looked me over as he approached me.

"Are you Mr. Nick McCord?" the police sergeant asked.

"Yes."

I noticed the other officer went around to the side of the house. I already knew what he was going to find.

"What's the problem?"

"I came here to talk to Mr. Billy Ricker. I rang the doorbell, but didn't get an answer. I noticed a light in the basement window when I pulled up. I walked around and looked in thinking that he might be in the basement and didn't hear the doorbell. I'm not sure, but I think that is Billy Ricker lying on the basement floor. I then called 9-1-1."

"There's a body on the floor in the basement, all right," the young officer said. "It looks like he's dead."

"Did you check the doors?"

"No," the officer said.

"Did you try the doors, Mr. McCord?"

"No. I didn't want to possibly destroy any evidence that might be found. Besides, I was pretty sure he was dead and there was nothing I could do for him."

"Don't go anywhere, either of you," the sergeant said as he glanced at Monica.

The sergeant went around to the back of the house then broke in. It was only a few minutes before he returned to where his partner was waiting with us.

"He's dead all right," the sergeant said. "Call in for a detective. Tell them we have a homicide."

The young office went to the patrol car and called it in. I could hear him requesting a detective and forensic team. He told them it was a homicide.

I knew it was going to be a long night. There was very little chance that we would be allowed to leave, and might even be taken to the precinct for questioning.

"Mr. McCord, would you mind telling me why you are here?"

"Not at all, but I should tell you who I am. I'm a private investigator from Madison, Wisconsin. I do have a gun. Can I reach in my pocket for my ID and permit to carry?"

"Yes," the sergeant said, then glanced at Monica.

"Is she licensed to carry?"

"No, she's my wife and partner, but not a licensed investigator, nor is she licensed to carry."

"Okay. Why are you here?"

"I'm working on a case where a race car driver was killed while driving his vintage Ferrari on a privately owned racetrack only about fifteen miles or so from here."

"I heard about that," the young officer said.

"The reason I am here is Billy Ricker was one of the racetrack's cleanup people. He called me to tell me he had some evidence that might help me prove one way or the other if it was murder. I was to meet him here, at his home, at eight o'clock for him to give me the evidence he found while cleaning up the track where the crash of the Ferrari took place."

"I read in the paper that the Chicago Police ruled the death an accident," the young office said.

"That is true," I said to the young officer.

"What was the evidence Mr. Ricker found," the sergeant asked.

"He claimed he had the ends of three bolts and a piece of metal from the crash. He had what I believe were the other ends of the bolts I had found still in the car when I inspected it. They were examined and found to be the wrong kind of bolts for what they had been used for.

"As for the piece of metal, I have no idea how, or if it had anything to do with the crash of the car."

"I get the impression that you don't know this Billy Ricker?"

"That would be correct. I have only talked to him on the phone. I've never met him in person."

It was a that moment that a sedan with a red flashing light on the dash pulled up in front of the house behind the patrol car. I watched as a man in a sport coat and slacks stepped out of the car and walk toward the sergeant. The two of them talked for several minutes. I noticed that the detective glanced over at me a couple of times while he was getting a brief report from the sergeant. I saw the detective nod his head then walk toward me.

"How the hell are you, Nick," Detective Joe Martin said as he stuck out his hand.

"Pretty good. How have you been, Joe?"

"Doing the same old job," he said. "Say, who's your partner?"

"Monica, this is Detective Joe Martin of the Calumet City Police Department. Joe, this is my wife and partner, Monica."

"Nice to meet you, Monica. I wish it had been under better circumstances."

"Nice to meet you, Detective."

"Please, call me, Joe. Nick and I go back a lot of years."

Monica looked at me.

"Joe and I worked together a few years back when we were both street cops in Milwaukee."

"Oh," Monica said with a smile.

"Back to business," Joe said. "Is there anything you can tell me that might help me find out who killed this guy?"

"I've told the sergeant about all I know. I was hired by Mrs. Brandon Smith to find out if her husband, Brandon, had been murdered in his vintage race car while racing it on a track near here. If what Billy Ricker told me over the phone was true, he might have had some evidence that would help determine if Brandon was murdered, or if it was an accident as the Chicago Police determined it to be. From what I have found so far, I'm inclined to think it was murder. The death of Ricker, sort of reinforces that belief."

"So, you think he was killed because he had evidence that might go a long way in proving it was murder?"

"Something like that, except I don't know if what he had meant anything at all to me."

"So, some of the things we should be looking for are three partial bolts and a piece of metal. Any idea of how big a piece of metal and what color it might be?"

"Sorry, Joe. I'm afraid I can't make it easy for you. If it is from the Ferrari, it would be my guess it would likely be red, but I have no idea what color it is, or how big the piece of metal might be. However, Ricker did say that the broken bolts still had the nuts on them."

"It might help for you to know that Ricker said he was taking the items home in his lunch box. I have no idea how big a lunch box he might have, but there is a chance that they are still in his lunch box, unless whoever killed him found them."

"That might help a little. Most lunch boxes are not all that big."

Just then the forensic team drove up. Joe looked at the van as it stopped in front of the driveway. I saw three members of the forensic team get out of the van.

"I've got to go to work. Please wait here," Joe said.

"We'll wait in the car," I said.

Joe nodded that he heard me, then headed toward the van to talk to the leader of the forensic team. Monica and I walked back to our car. We got in, then relaxed. It was going to take a while before they would be finished.

We sat in the car and watched what was going on. We couldn't see much, but every once in a while someone would bring an evidence bag out of the house and put it in the van. We had no idea what was in the bags, but it was something they must have thought was important, or might even be remotely considered evidence.

We had been sitting in the car for about an hour when I noticed Joe walking toward us. He looked like someone who had bad news. I got out of the car and waited for him to come to me.

Sorry, Nick. We haven't found the bolts or the piece of metal, and there's no lunch box. It would be my guess that whoever killed him took it with them."

"You said, 'them'. Does that mean you think there was more than one person involved in Ricker's death?"

"It sure looks that way. He was beaten pretty bad. From the looks of the injuries, someone held him while someone else worked him over. It also looked like it started on the main floor of the house. He was then taken to the basement where he was shot in the head. The upstairs looks like it had been searched, and it has all the signs that someone knew what they were looking for," Joe said.

"Since he was worked over, it seems logical that the thugs must have thought what he found could implicate them in causing the crash, or implicate whoever the thugs worked for in causing the death of Brandon."

"That would certainly explain why he was killed," Joe said.

"The forensic team is just really getting started processing the scene. It's a mess and will be awhile before we know what they find."

"You might want your people to check out the garage. If Ricker's car is in the garage, he might have left his lunch box in the car, or possibly in the garage."

"Don't know if they thought of that, but I'll certainly let them know to check it out."

"Thanks, Joe. Do you need us anymore?"

"No. Besides, I know where to find you if we come up with anything that might help you, or if I have any questions for you," Joe said.

"Here's my card. If you need me just call. I think we'll return home. I don't think there is anything more we can do here."

"Probably not. I'll call you and let you know what we find. If we find the bolts and that piece of metal, I'll be sure to call you."

Thanks, Joe. It was good to see you again."

"Take care going home. Nice to have met you, Monica."

Monica smiled from the car. I walked around and got into the car. I glanced toward the house as I started the car. I wondered what the forensic team was going to find.

I pulled out onto the street. Once we were on the road, Monica looked over at me.

"What's on your mind, Honey?"

"I was thinking. Why would someone kill Ricker when they already know that we have the top part of the bolts? It doesn't make sense."

"It might, if it is the piece of metal Ricker claimed to have found, and not the bolts, that could connect someone to the tampering of the car's suspension.

"You have a good point there."

"We don't know what the piece of metal has to do with anything since we don't know where it is from, what purpose it served, and what role it might have played in the crash," I said.

"Ricker calling it a piece of metal indicates that he didn't know anything about it, himself."

"That is probably a good assumption," Monica agreed. "What do we do now?"

"I think we should head for home. I don't think there is anything more we can do tonight. I want to make a few phone calls tomorrow. One of them to the Chicago Police Department. I want to talk to the accident investigator."

"Do you really think he can provide any additional information?"

"I don't know. I want to call Professor Houzerman to see what he might have found out."

Monica leaned back in her seat as I drove. We headed for home and it would take us until after midnight to get there. I had to admit it had been a long day, with little to show for it.

The question of why was Billy Ricker killed stuck in my mind. Did he know more than he had indicated when I talked to him on the phone? Did he know who had rigged the car to crash, or who shot the tire? These were questions that I doubted would get answered anytime soon, if at all.

Another thought came to mind. I knew it was hard to shoot out a tire of a fast moving vehicle. Was the grove in the race track actually caused by a bullet? If it was, was whoever fired the shot trying to hit a tire? Another look at the car might just be in order.

With all that had happened, I continued to watch for anyone who might be following us. I didn't want to get caught unaware of my surroundings and end up in a ditch somewhere.

CHAPTER ELEVEN

The drive home from Calumet City was uneventful. I didn't see anyone following us. We arrived home just shortly before midnight. As soon as I pulled up in front of the garage and stopped, Monica sat up. She had dozed off.

"Are we home?" Monica said as she looked around.

"Yes. I want you to stay here while I make sure there is no one hanging around our apartment."

Monica looked at me. I could see by the expression on her face that she was worried.

"Just stay in the car. This won't take long."

"Be careful."

"I will."

I took my gun out from under my coat and held it close to my side while I walked toward our apartment. When I got to the top of the staircase and turned to go into our apartment, I heard a door open behind me. I quickly turned and saw Mr. Robert Jackson stick his head out of his apartment.

"Good evening, Bob," I said, as I slipped my gun under my coat. "You're up rather late, aren't you?"

"A little. I've been waiting for you to come home."

"Oh. Why? Has something happened?"

"I'm not sure, but there was someone at the door to your apartment; and he seemed rather insistent on seeing you. He was knocking on your door rather hard. Since it was after dark, I thought you ought to know."

"Who was it?"

"I don't know, but since I knew the police had been here, and that you shot a man trying to break into your apartment, I thought it might be important for you to know who the guy was that was pounding on your door."

"You don't know who it was?"

"No, but I took a picture of him."

"You have a picture of him?"

"Yes. I printed it off on my computer for you."

Bob handed me the photograph. I looked at it. I found it interesting. It was a photo of Josh Ellis, Barbara Smith's personal assistant. I wondered what he wanted, and why he had come to our apartment so late.

"Do you know this man?" Bob asked.

"Yes. As a matter of fact, I do. Did you talk to him?"

"Yes. I took the picture, then quickly put my camera back in my apartment. I didn't want him to know I had taken his picture. I asked him what he wanted."

"What did he have to say?"

"He said that he worked for the person who had hired you, and that he was here to see if you had made any progress in your investigation."

"Did you believe him?"

"Not for a minute. If he was working for the person who had hired you, it seemed more logical that person would simply call you if that was all they wanted to know. And why would he come at such a late hour?"

"Good thinking. What did you tell him?"

"I told him I know nothing about any investigation. I also told him that I know you are an investigator, but that was about all I knew about you."

"Did that seem to satisfy him?"

"I don't think so. He did ask if I knew when you would be home. I told him that I had no idea when you would be home, or where you went, and that all I knew about you is you are some kind of an investigator, but I didn't know who or what you might be investigating. I also mentioned that your wife was a college professor, but didn't know what department she worked in. Of course, I do know that she no longer works for the university, and she is working with you."

"Was there anything else?"

"No. He thanked me, then turned and left. I got the feeling he didn't believe me, but he didn't say so. I watched from my apartment window to make sure he left the complex."

"Did he leave the complex right away?"

"No. He sat in his car for about fifteen minutes before he drove off in a fairly new red Corvette. I don't know the year of those kind of cars, but it was not very old, not more than about two, maybe three years old, at the most."

"Thanks for the information, Bob. That was good work on your part. You want a job as an investigator?" I said with a smile.

"No, but thanks anyway."

Bob smiled, nodded, then turned and went back into his apartment. I glanced at the photograph. What did Josh really want with me? Did he tell Bob the truth, that he was just interested in knowing if we were making any progress in our investigation? Like Bob, I had my doubts. After all, it was about a half a day's drive from Calumet City to our place. Josh probably left because he knew that our neighbor was watching our apartment, and would probably report to me that Josh had been there.

I drew my gun from under my coat, then opened the door to our apartment. I took my time entering. I reached around the corner and turned on the light. I saw nothing unusual. As soon as I had been through the entire apartment and found nothing out of order, I returned to the garage for Monica.

"What took you so long? I was getting worried," Monica asked as we walked to our apartment.

"We had a visitor earlier. Josh Ellis came by. Our neighbor took a picture of him at our door," I said.

I waited to tell her about my visit with Bob until we were in our apartment. I showed her the picture. On the back of the picture, Bob had written the date and time he had taken the picture, as well as the location of the picture.

"I just might have to hire Bob to keep an eye on our place. He seems to know when to take pictures, and knows enough to put important information on the back as to where and when it was taken.

"Are you serious?" Monica asked.

"Not really. I don't want him doing something that might cause him problems. You have to admit that it was nice of him to take the photograph rather than to rely on his memory to give me a good description of Josh."

"That was good thinking on his part," Monica admitted.

I was just about to sit down for a few minutes to check out the news when the phone in our office began to ring. I went into the office and picked up the phone.

"McCord Investigative Agency, how may I help you?"

"Hi, Nick. This is Joe, Joe Martin. I hope I didn't wake you. I was hoping to get you before you went to bed."

"We just got in. We were going to check the news. What's up."

"I got a feeling that Mr. Ricker knew a lot more about the items he had, and you wanted, than he was telling you."

"What makes you think that?"

"We found his lunch box in the pantry in the kitchen. It was probably where he usually kept it when he wasn't using it. It was empty. However, when we searched the garage, we found a plain brown paper sack on top of a cabinet. If we hadn't been looking for it, we probably would have missed it. It didn't look like it had anything in it. One of the forensic guys took hold of it. It felt heavy, way too heavy to be empty, so he opened it. The bag contained three partial bolts with nuts on them, and a small piece of metal.

"Ricker must have had some idea that it was important or he wouldn't have hidden it. It seems logical to assume he was afraid someone would be looking for it," Joe explained.

"I would say that he had reason to believe it was important. I only wish I knew why he thought it was so important that he took the time and effort to hide it."

"So do I. If we had the answer to that, we would probably be able to find out who killed him."

"Did you find any evidence that would point you to who killed him?"

"We found a lot of fingerprints, and some blood in the kitchen and bedroom, as well as in the basement. We don't know whose fingerprints they are, yet. We're still checking that out.

"The blood on the basement floor was obviously Ricker's. He had been shot in the head. From the blood splatter on the walls, he was shot in the basement. From the look of his face, he must have taken one hell of a beating. The blood in the kitchen and bedroom is probably Ricker's, but we are having it tested to be sure.

"We did find some blood in the bathroom sink just off the bedroom, and a towel in the waste basket under the sink with blood on it. That may not have been Ricker's. It is possible that it is from one of his attackers. It looked like someone had used the towel to stop bleeding on his hands.

"The bedroom looks like Ricker might have put up a fight. Cuts on his hands indicate that he might have hit back at least a couple of times."

"Thanks for the information. What are the chances of getting the partial bolts and the piece of metal to me?" I asked.

"I talked to my captain. I told him of your background as a police detective and our friendship. I also told him about your expert at the university and that you would be glad to work with us. At no cost to our department, I might add.

"I got him to agree to get all the items to you, if, and I say IF, you will agree to share with us what your expert tells you about them. I assured him that you would share that information with us. I hope I didn't stick my neck out on this one."

"Not at all. I will gladly share information with you in the hope you will share information about what your people gather with me."

"No problem there. We'll share what we find out with you."

"By the way, the tests on the bolts and piece of metal will be in writing and signed by the expert who will test them. I will see to it you get a certified copy of his reports on the bolts and the piece of metal as well as on the items he has already tested for me on this case. Since he is an expert on the subject, his reports should hold up in court, if it comes to that," I said.

"Good. I'll tell my captain that we have a deal. By the way, I took pictures of the bolts and the piece of metal. I used a ruler to show their size."

"Great. Send me copies of the pictures, and keep me posted on what you find. I'll keep you posted on what I find."

"Okay. Talk to you later," Joe said then hung up.

I turned to see Monica standing in the doorway to the office. She had a smile on her face.

"I take it you got the gist of my conversation with Joe Martin?"

"Yes. It's good to have a little help on this one."

"It sure is."

"I think it is time to get some sleep. I'm going to take a shower. Would you care to join me?" Monica said with a smile.

"I would love to shower with you."

It didn't take us very long to get out of our clothes and into the shower. We spent a lot longer in the shower than what would normally be needed, but it was an enjoyable time for both of us.

Once out of the shower and dried off, we climbed into bed, but we didn't go to sleep right away. We spent a good hour making love and enjoying each other. It was a time to just share ourselves with each other. It wasn't long after our love making before we fell asleep in each other's arms.

CHAPTER TWELVE

Morning came much earlier than I had hoped. My day started with the ringing of the telephone in the office. I rolled away from Monica, slid out of bed and ran to the office. I picked up the phone, but I was still half asleep.

"McCord Detective Agency," I managed to say.

"I strongly suggest that you give up your investigation of the death of Brandon Smith, and leave it an accident," a rough voice said, then the phone went dead.

Needless to say, I was wide awake now. I sat down in my chair as I hung up the phone. I sat there and thought about what had been said. I tried to hear the voice in my head again and again in an effort to figure out if I had heard that voice before. I knew whoever he was, he was trying to disguise his voice so I wouldn't recognize it. That could mean if he spoke to me in his normal voice, I would probably recognize his voice and know who it was that called. There was also the possibility he was trying to make himself sound tougher than he really might be with a goal of getting me to give up my investigation without further action required on his part.

If my last thought was his goal, he didn't know me very well. I don't like to be threatened, and take it very personal. It also makes me think that someone is getting very concerned that I am getting too close to the truth.

"Who was that?" Monica said.

I turned and looked at her standing in the doorway. She looked like she was still half asleep. She was wearing her robe.

"I don't know. All he said was to drop our investigation of Brandon's death. It was obviously a threat."

"Oh. You should get something on."

"I will, as soon as I get back to the bedroom."

"Are you going back to bed?" Monica asked.

"I'm awake now. You can go back to bed if you like. It's still pretty early."

"If you're getting up, I guess I will, too."

"I'll get dressed and fix us a good breakfast."

"Okay."

I got out of my chair and walked back to the bedroom with her. As soon as I was dressed, I went to the kitchen and began fixing breakfast. All the time I was fixing it, the voice from the phone was running over and over through my head like a stuck record. By the time breakfast was ready, I had a pretty good idea who it might have been, but I wasn't a hundred percent sure.

"Is breakfast ready?" Monica asked as she entered the kitchen.

"It will be in a minute. Sit down."

I served up a breakfast of eggs, a ham slice, and toast with coffee and orange juice. I sat down across from Monica and looked at her. She was the most beautiful woman I could ever remember seeing.

"What are you thinking?" she asked.

"I was thinking about how beautiful you are."

"Thank you."

We commenced eating breakfast. Nothing much was said until we were almost done. We had been deep in thought. I was sure Monica was thinking about the threatening phone call earlier this morning.

I had been thinking about the call, too. Only I was still trying to think of why the person I thought had called would want me to drop my investigation. It made no sense to me.

"What are you thinking about now?" Monica asked.

"The phone call this morning."

"Me, too. Do you have some idea who might be the person making that call?" Monica asked.

"Yes, but it doesn't make any sense."

"Who do you think it was?"

"Remember the guard at the back gate of the Smith estate?"

"Yes. His name was Neal Upton, I believe. Do you think he made the call?"

"Yes, I think it was him. Even though he tried to sound different, the caller had the same speech pattern as Neil Upton. Oh, his voice was much lower and he said the words with a bit of authority in them, but it all sounded forced like he had rehearsed it a number of times before calling. It also sounded like he was uncomfortable saying it."

"Why would he call us like that?" Monica asked.

"I doubt he would have done that on his own."

"I agree."

"Someone either talked him into doing it, or paid him to do it."

"Or threatened him with something to do it," Monica added.

"That's a possibility, too. But why?"

"If he was paid to do it, he might have needed the money."

"That's a possibility, too. I don't know why or who put him up to it, but I plan to find out."

"Do you know where the call came from?" she asked.

"There's no phone number or name on the caller ID. That might mean that he called from an unlisted cell phone."

"What are you going to do now?" Monica asked.

"As soon as I clean up the kitchen, I'm going to spend the next couple of hours doing background checks on all of those who we know have some relationship, either working or personal, to Brandon Smith. I'll also try to get credit checks and financial reports on them as well. This will probably take most of the day."

"What do you want me to do? I don't really want to sit here and watch you work."

"Would you call Professor Houzerman and see what he found out from the scrapings I took from the floor of the

Ferrari that I asked him to analyze? I would like to know what it is. It looked like blood to me."

"I'll call him now."

"You might let him know that we think we have the ends to the bolts he has, and a piece of metal we would like him to analyze for us. Let him know we will get them to him as soon as we get them from the Calumet City police."

Monica nodded that she understood then sat down at her desk in the office. She placed a call to Professor Houzerman's office while I started to work on getting reports on my suspects.

Her call was put through very quickly. Although I could not hear the professor's response to Monica's questions, and what she told him about the new evidence, it sounded like he had determined what the scrapings were.

Just as Monica was hanging up, the background check on Russell Larson came up on my computer screen. Monica didn't say anything while I looked at Russell's background check.

After reading a portion of the background check on Larson, I decided it would be a good idea to print it out so I could sit down and go through it bit by bit. I pressed the button to print it out, then turned to Monica.

"What did the professor have to say?"

"He said that the scrapings you gave him was definitely dried human blood. He also said that it was too degraded to get any good information on it. It had probably been where you found it for some time, but it was hard to tell. He also said there were traces of oil and dirt in the sample you gave him."

"That's one piece of evidence that doesn't help us."

"Not everything we find is evidence," she reminded me.

"That's true. What did he say about our new evidence?"

"He said he would be glad to look at it as soon as you get it to him."

"Good. I had a thought. See what you can find on Smith Steel Fabrication Company. I want to know everything there is to know about the company, who owns it, who has a piece of it, in other words, everything you can think of."

"Sure. Do you think that Brandon has some silent partners?" Monica asked.

"I don't know, but it doesn't hurt to find out."

"I'll get started."

"I'll continue to do background checks on our suspect list. If you come up with any names we don't already have, let me know. I'll run a background check on them, too."

"Okay."

It was getting on toward lunchtime when I finally had background checks on all the people we knew were, or might be, involved with Brandon in some way, even in some small way. Rather than try to read the background checks on the computer, I had printed them off so I could sit down and take my time looking over each one for any clues that might be there.

"How are you doing over there?" I asked Monica.

"I'm not sure. The one thing I have found out is that Brandon didn't own very much of Smith Steel Fabrication Company. From what I can gather, small pieces of the company had been sold off to another company over the past almost three years."

"Were they sold off to just one company?"

"Yes. It does appear to be only one company."

"What is the name of the other company?"

"W.S. and S. Corporation. I've never heard of them," Monica said.

"I'll see if I can find them."

I began looking for the company. It didn't take me long to discover it was a company with its headquarters in the Cayman Islands. The information on the company was limited to the fact it existed, and that was about it. It appeared that it was not a corporation. There were no officers of the company listed. I quickly got the idea that it just might be a shell company. In other words, it wasn't a company at all, but a place to hide money while keeping ownership of the money private, as well as where it came from. It made nothing and sold nothing. It was simply a place to hide money offshore away from the eyes of any government, especially the U. S Government.

"I found the company in the Cayman Islands. It doesn't list any of the officers of the company. I was hoping we would be able to find out who W.S. and S are."

"What now?"

"We keep looking. After lunch, I'm going to sit down and go over all these background reports I've printed off and see if anything pops out at me."

Monica and I put up what we had been working on. We went to the kitchen and made lunch. We didn't talk much at lunch. I know I had a lot on my mind, and I was sure she did as well.

Just as we finished lunch, there was a knock on the door. We looked at each other. I stood up, went to the bedroom and picked up my gun off the nightstand before going to the door.

Before I opened the door, I looked to see if Monica was out of sight. She had gone to the office and closed the door. I turned around, took hold of the door knob and opened the door. Standing in front of the door was Joe Martin.

"You expecting trouble?" he asked when he saw the gun in my hand.

"I certainly wasn't expecting you. The way things have been shaping up, it is a strong possibility. Come on in."

Joe walked into our apartment, then watched me as I looked around outside the door. I didn't see anything that might be of concern to me.

"Monica, it's all clear. It's Joe Martin."

Monica came out of the office and smiled at Joe.

"What brings you here?" I asked.

"I decided that it might be better if I brought over the evidence we found in Ricker's house. I didn't want to mail it to you in case someone might get their hands on it before you."

"Let's take a look at it."

Joe handed the sack to me, then followed me to the kitchen table. I set the sack on the table then looked at Joe.

"Have your people checked them for fingerprints?"

"Yes, but they didn't have the results before I left. I'll call you when I get it."

I opened the sack and looked inside. There were three partial bolts with nuts on them and a small piece of metal. I reached in the sack and took out the piece of metal. I carefully looked it over, turning it over several times in my hands. I couldn't figure out where it came from. It was red, possibly Ferrari red, but I wasn't sure. It had a number of scratches on one side. They looked like scratches that would be the result of scraping on the asphalt or concrete pavement, possibly when it came off the car. It also had some scratches from possibly a screwdriver or other tool used to try to pry it loose.

"Any idea what it is?" Joe asked, interrupting my thoughts.

"No. The red color looks like Ferrari red to me, but I can't be sure. The Ferrari dealer in Chicago might know what it is and what is it used for."

"I hadn't thought about that." Joe said.

I also looked at the pictures that Joe had taken. They were clear and had a ruler in them that showed the size of the piece of metal. It was six inches long and three and a half inches wide, with rounded corners.

"These pictures will help a lot. I'll show them to the parts department of the Ferrari dealership in Chicago. They might be able to tell us what the bolts were used for and where on the car the piece of metal is from."

"Let me know what you find out."

"I will. Could you run me an arrest record on a couple of people?"

"Sure. Who do you want it on?" Joe asked.

"Four people, Russell Larson, Billy Ricker, Josh Ellis and Neal Upton."

"Anything I should know about them?

"Larson, Ellis and Upton work for Barbara Smith, or the company she owns. Of course, you know Ricker worked for the racetrack where Brandon died."

"Okay. I'll let you know. Right now, I need to get back. I'll send you the reports on all of them."

"Thanks for bringing these things for me. Drive safe."

"I will. It's nice to see you again, Monica."

"It was nice of you to personally bring us the evidence."

"You're welcome."

Joe turned and left the apartment. I went to the window in the living room and watched Joe get into his car. As he left the parking lot, I watched to see if anyone might be following him, or seemed to take an interest in him. I saw no one.

I also looked around to see if there might be someone in the parking lot that didn't live in the complex. I didn't see anyone.

Monica and I returned to our office. I picked up the phone and called the Parts Department of the Chicago Ferrari Dealership. I told the Parts Department supervisor what I had. I described the piece of metal to him, but he was unable to tell me what it was. He suggested that I send him copies of the pictures of the item, and he would get back to me as soon as possible.

As soon as I got his e-mail address, I scanned the pictures Joe had given me into my computer, then e-mailed the pictures along with a note to the dealership. All I could do now was wait for a reply.

CHAPTER THIRTEEN

While I waited for the response to the e-mail I sent to the Ferrari Dealership in Chicago, I sat down at a table and laid out the first background check. I started with Russell Larson. I carefully read over the entire report. I was surprised to find that Russell had served time at Joliet Prison in Illinois for theft of auto parts from the sports car dealership in Chicago where he had worked for several years.

He had worked at the dealership as a mechanic, and took parts from the dealership to fix cars he worked on in his home garage, charging for the parts he used in repairing those cars, plus labor. However, he didn't pay the dealership for the parts he used. Instead, he pocketed the money. He had served two years and seven months of a four-year sentence.

It was the only black mark I found on his record. Other than the prison time, his background check had nothing else of any interest to me.

Russell's employment after his jail time was a mechanic for Smith Steel Fabrications. His job there was to maintain the machines used in the plant. There was no indication in the report that he had been hired to work on Brandon's car. Yet, we know for a fact that he did work on the car, because he was Brandon's chief mechanic. I could only assume that Brandon knew of his past, but hired him anyway, and then had him help with his vintage Ferrari because of his knowledge of sports cars.

"Monica, it looks like Russell spent some time in jail. Do you have his financial report and credit report?"

"Yes. Russell's financial report and credit report shows he is in debt up to his neck. He has two credit cards and both are maxed out, and a loan that he should not have gotten based on his credit and income. He doesn't own the house he lives in. It belongs to his mother. Apparently, the house was used as collateral for the loan."

"Is there any indication that his mother co-signed for the loan?"

"No, but that doesn't mean she didn't," Monica said as she looked at me. "There's just nothing in the reports to show she, or anyone else, had co-signed for the loan. Her name doesn't show up on the loan information."

"That's strange. I can't see a bank making a loan without proper collateral."

"I'm not sure the loan was from a bank. There's no loan application form from a bank. It may have been a private party loan, but it doesn't show who made the loan to him."

I sat back and thought about what we had on Russell. There was nothing to point to him as having anything to do with Brandon's death. However, there might be something in his background and finances that could be used by someone to force him to participate in fixing Brandon's car so it would crash.

I put up Russell's background check for now. I had a lot of suspects to think about, Russell was only one of them.

I picked up the next background check. It was on Neal Upton, one of the gate guards at the Smith Estate.

"What about the gate guard, Neal Upton?" I asked.

"His credit record and financial report are not any better than Russell's. He is also in hock up to his neck. I do see that he has a rather large loan owed to William F. Stoker. Isn't that the guy that Martin told us about?"

"No. We heard about him from Lieutenant Gerrie Baker. She warned us about him. He is rich, and has a lot of influence with judges and lawyers."

"Oh. I remember. He also has several vintage cars."

"Yes, that's him."

"Is he on your list of people you wanted to get background checks on?"

"Not on my original list, but he is on it now."

I added Stoker to my list of suspects. For the life of me, I don't know how I missed him as a suspect. I was sure he had a number of reasons to want to see Brandon out of the vintage car shows, and I wouldn't put it past someone like him to get rid of the competition by killing them. However, there might be some other reason for wanting Brandon dead.

I pulled up a background check on my computer of one William F. Stoker, of Chicago, Illinois. It took a while for it to come up. It was a rather lengthy file which would take some time to read it all. That was all the more reason to read it carefully. While it was printing, I turned my attention to one of my other suspects.

I picked up the background check on Josh Ellis. The first thing I noticed was he was only twenty-four years old. His background check showed he had a master's degree in business and finance, and according to his school records graduated in the top ten percent of his class. From having talked to him, I thought he was smart, but this showed me just how smart he really was. This bit of information caused me to think about why was he playing the role of personal assistant to Barbara Smith since he was more than qualified to work in almost any business that used people with his education. He didn't really have much of a background to check. It appeared that working for Barbara Smith was his first and only job after college.

Monica had mentioned at one time that Josh might be more than a personal assistant to Barbara. Barbara had to be at least fifteen years his senior. Even at over forty, Barbara was a very attractive woman. The picture it brought to mind caused me to wonder what was really going on between them, what were his duties as a "personal assistant"?

"Nick?"

"Yes."

"I found something that might interest you."

"What have you got?"

"William Stoker has a business in the Cayman Islands."

"That is interesting. You think he might be the 'W.S.' in the W.S. and S. Company?"

"I think he might be the 'W.S.' in the company. What I found indicates there are only two people who own that company," Monica said.

"I wonder who the other 'S' is?" I asked, thinking out loud.

"I don't know, but if I had to guess, it might be Smith, as in Barbara Smith."

"What gives you that idea?"

"It's just a thought, on my part." Monica admitted.

"Keep digging. It might just be more than a thought. See what you can find on her."

I watched Monica as she turned back to her computer. There was no doubt in my mind that Monica was not only beautiful, she was smart. But I already knew that. I was sure that she could find everything there was to know about Barbara Smith.

I turned back to start looking at another background check I had printed out when a message came up on my screen telling me that I had an e-mail coming in. I turned over to my e-mail files. There was a message from the Ferrari Dealership in Chicago. I brought the message up on my computer.

The message reads: *"The photo of the piece of metal you sent indicates that the piece of metal is not from a Ferrari. I showed it to one of our body men who has done a lot of work on vintage cars. He thinks it might be from an American car, possibly from a Packard from the early 1930s, probably a 1931 or 1932 Packard. He thought it looked like a metal plate that was used to cover an access hole in the firewall behind the dash.*

The scraping on the metal piece was probably from someone using a screwdriver to take it off. He said some of the panel covers were hard to get off. I hope this is of some help. Let me know if we can be of any further assistance."

It was signed by the Parts Department Supervisor.

The e-mail caused more questions than it answered. If it wasn't from the Ferrari, how did it get on the racetrack? My next question was, who owned an early nineteen-thirties Packard? It suddenly occurred to me that the list of entries to the Concourse De'Alligance show would probably answer that last question.

I started looking for information on the most recent Concourse De'Alligance Show in Chicago, Illinois. Once I found it, I went straight to the list of the cars that were entered in the show. I found that there were five Packards from the years 1930 to 1940. Of the five cars, two were 1930 Packard Le Baron models, one 1931 Packard Brewster, a 1934 Packard Le Baron Town Car and one 1940 Packard Sedan. When I looked at who owned the cars, I was not surprised to find that William F. Stoker owned two of them, one of the 1930 Le Barons, and the other was the 1934 Le Baron Town Car. I also noticed that only one of them was red. It was the 1930 Le Baron owned by Stoker. It was red and cream colored.

I told Monica what I had found out. She wasn't surprised either. The next thing for me to do was to take a close look at Stoker's background check as well as a financial report, credit report, and criminal report. It also might not be a bad idea to look at how the cars owned by Stoker did in the show.

I went straight to the results of the show on the web site. I was not surprised that Stoker's two Packards took first and second place in their category. I also noticed that a 1954 4.9 Mille Miglia Ferrari took first place in its class and Best of Show. That car was Brandon's Ferrari.

My search of several other Concourse De'Alligance Shows around the country, showed me that Brandon Smith's Ferrari beat out Stoker's Packards for Best of Show at four of the five shows listed. It happened that three of the four best of show wins by Brandon were in the last three shows

Brandon's Ferrari was entered in. It was time to take a good look at Stoker's background check.

I knew it would take a while to get the rest of the reports I wanted on Stoker, especially the criminal report. A call to Lieutenant Gerrie Baker might save me some time. She had already told me that he had a rather lengthy criminal record. If she would cooperate with me, I would probably get information that might not show up in a routine criminal check. I wanted to know all the things he had been arrested for, and what the outcome was in each case.

"Monica, I'm going to give Lieutenant Baker a call. I would like to see Stoker's criminal record. She might be able to get it for me."

"Did you find something?"

"I did. It seems that Stoker lost out on Best of Show at several Concourse De'Alligance Shows around the country to Brandon's Ferrari. I have a feeling that he might be the kind of a man who would do anything to win."

"She might be able to tell us something about his temperament as well," Monica suggested.

"That's part of what I'm hoping to find out."

I reached out and picked up the phone. I placed a call to Lieutenant Baker. It didn't take but a couple of minutes for her to answer the phone.

"Good afternoon, Nick. How may I help you?"

"Lieutenant, . . . "

"I think you can call me, Gerrie," she said interrupting me.

"Okay, Gerrie. I was hoping that you could provide me with the criminal records on William F. Stoker."

"I take it you have something on him?"

"I'm not sure, but I have at least one, possibly two, motives for him wanting Brandon Smith dead."

"What are these two motives?"

"Jealousy, for one. He may very well be jealous of Brandon because in several Concourse De'Alligance Shows around the country, he has lost Best of Show to Brandon's vintage Ferrari. I believe he might be the type of person who would not stand for that very long.

"The other motive is a little more complicated. Brandon may have found out that Stoker has been buying up pieces of his business over the past three or more years without his knowledge, and that Stoker now owns a majority of his company."

There was silence on the other end of the line. I had a pretty good idea that Gerrie was thinking about what I told her.

"Are you sure about this?"

"Not one hundred percent sure, but everything I have been able to find out, so far, certainly points in that direction."

Again, there was silence on the line.

"What is it you think you will find in his criminal records?"

"I'm not sure. The one thing I'm hoping to find out is what sort of things make him angry, and how he deals with those things and his anger."

"I see your point, but he is out of my jurisdiction. I don't really have much on Mr. Stoker."

"I understand that, but as a police officer, you would be able to get his complete criminal records from the Chicago Police Department. Besides, the two thugs that broke into my apartment were connected to him. That would be reason enough to get his records."

"That's true. However, I would not be able to give it to you."

"That's also true, but maybe you could let me read it in your office. They would be more favorable in sending it to you since you are investigating the two men who tried to break into our apartment," I said, hoping she would help us.

"You have a point there. I'll request the information you want, but your only access to it will be here in my office, and I will be present when you look at it.

"That is fine with me."

"Okay, I'll send for it," she said.

"Thanks. Let me know when you get it."

"I will," Gerrie said then hung up."

I smiled to myself as I hung up the phone.

"I take it she is going to get Stoker's criminal record for you?" Monica asked.

"Yes, she is. I'll only be able to see it in her office."

"That's okay, isn't it?"

"Sure. I'm pretty lucky to get to see it at all."

"What now?"

"I think we should get the evidence Joe brought over to Professor Houzerman. I'd like to be able to find out what it means."

"A break from all this paperwork would be nice," Monica admitted.

We closed down our computers and put away all the information we had gathered, locking it up in a safe we have in the closet. Once we were ready, we left the apartment and headed for the University of Wisconsin Department of Engineering.

CHAPTER FOURTEEN

We arrived at the University of Wisconsin Department of Engineering shortly before four in the afternoon. We had the bag I received from Joe containing the small metal plate and the partial bolts with the nuts still on them.

As we entered Professor Houzerman's outer office, we saw him talking to his secretary. He had his coat on as if he was ready to leave.

"Professor, are we too late to have a talk with you?" I asked.

He turned and looked at us. He smiled.

"No. I always have time to talk to you. What can I do for you today?"

"I have what I think are the other half of the bolts you already have, and a piece of metal I would like you to examine."

I gave him the bag with the items in it. I watched him as he opened the bag and looked inside. He looked up at me.

"Do you know anything about this piece of metal?"

"We think it is from a 1930 Packard Le Baron. It was reported to us that it was found on the racetrack where Brandon Smith's Ferrari crashed. We have no idea how it got there, or why it was there since there wasn't a Packard in the race."

"How do you know it is from a Packard?"

"I guess we really don't know for sure, but we were told that by a body man who has worked on vintage cars. He said it looked like it was an access plate on the firewall of a Packard. Access to what, I have no idea."

"I have some serious doubts about what you were told. I'll look into it just to make sure."

"I would appreciate it very much."

"It will take me a few days. I should be able to have a complete report on all the items I have examined, plus these, for you by the end of the week."

"That would be great, Professor. And thanks for your help."

"You might not be so thankful when you get my bill," he said with a grin.

"Whatever you charge, I'm sure your expertise will be worth every penny."

"Thank you for the vote of confidence."

"We'll get out of here so you can do what you have to do. Again, thanks."

"You're welcome, and Monica, don't be a stranger," he said.

"I'll try not to be," she said with a smile.

Monica and I left the professor's office and returned to our car. As I was ready to start the car, I looked over at Monica.

"Do you think he would like you to return to the university?"

"I wouldn't be surprised, but I'm not ready to do that."

"Does that mean you have been thinking about it?"

"I did for a brief time when we thought I was pregnant. I like working with you. Being a detective is a lot like what I did at the university, only different. The people I have investigated while at the university had been dead for a very long time, not just a few hours, or a few days."

"You're right. Sometimes you have very little to go on now. In old cases, like you investigated as a professor, there is often no one to question. You had to go with what evidence you had at hand," I said.

"That is sometimes the circumstances in the cases we work on, too," she reminded me.

I had to agree with her. I started the car and drove out of the parking lot. We decided to stop off at a restaurant for dinner before returning to our apartment.

Our conversation during dinner was mostly about Stoker, what we knew about him, and what we hoped to find out about him. Since we had so little information on him at this time, most of what was said was pure speculation.

As soon as we finished dinner, we returned to our apartment. Once again, I was cautious about entering our apartment. I found nothing to indicate that anyone had been in our apartment, and no one was in it now.

As soon as Monica had joined me in the apartment, we settled in to watch a little news. There was very little in the news of interest to us, and it had been a long day. We decided it was time to go to bed.

Just as I was getting up off the couch, the phone in our office began to ring. I walked over to the office and picked up the phone.

"McCord Detective Agency, how may I help you?

"You don't hear so good. This is your last warnin'. Drop your investigation or somethin' might happen to that lovely wife of yours," then the phone went dead before I could respond.

I hung up the phone, then sat there looking at it. It was time to get Monica some place where she would be safe, but where she could go and still work on the case. It would be easy to find a place where she could use her computer to dig into the backgrounds of our suspects. The only problem I had was convincing her that she was still a very important part of our investigation even if she was not with me.

I turned and looked toward the door. Monica was standing in the doorway looking at me.

"That was another threatening call, wasn't it?"

"Yes," I said.

I put my finger over my lips to let Monica know not to say anything more. I motioned her to come with me. I took her by the arm and walked with her to the front door of our apartment. After making sure no one could see us, we left the apartment and walked down the hall to the laundry room.

Once inside, I checked to make sure there was no one else in the room before I said anything.

"I think we need to find a place that is safer."

"Why are we here, do you think our apartment might be bugged?"

"Yes. That call was placed at just the time we were home. The caller ID didn't show anyone had tried to call us at any other time. He knew we were home. We need a place where we are not as vulnerable as we are here."

"I have an uncle who lives on a farm outside of Westfield, a little north of Portage. I would think it would be safe there, but it would put us a long way from where our suspects live."

"I'm thinking of some place where you would be safe, but where you could still work on the case with me. A place where no one would expect us to go."

"I would think my uncle's farm would be safe."

"It might be, but it would be rather easy for whoever called to figure that out. It has to be some place where you would not be connected to whoever owns where you are hiding."

"And just where would that be?" Monica asked.

"I need you to do the searching for information on our suspects, and research any other information we might need, or you might discover. You can do that from just about any place you can use a computer. I need you to do the research."

"And what will you be doing?"

"I will be contacting those that I need to contact, and checking out any information you might come across. I will do the leg work. I will also move around a lot so I'm not in one place very long. I will still keep in touch."

"Do you have an idea where this secret place might be?"

"What about Tom Walker's lodge near Gill's Rock. I'm sure Tom would put you up there. You would be able to work from his lodge at Gill's Point."

"Are you thinking of sending me there?"

"Yes, but only until I can find out who we are dealing with, and end any more threats to you."

"I don't like it."

"I'm sure you don't. I don't like it either."

"While I'm sitting safely in the lodge, what are you going to do?"

"I'm going to find out who is threatening us and put a stop to it. It will be harder for me to find out if I'm worried about you being safe."

Monica leaned back against the washing machine while just looking at me. I was sure that she was thinking about what I had said. I only hoped she could see the logic in it.

"Okay," she finally said. "Give Tom a call. If he can put me up, I'll go and wait for you there; but you have to stay in touch with me, often."

"I'm not going to call him from here. Our phone might be tapped or our apartment bugged, maybe both. Whoever is threatening us has had ample time to get into our apartment and bug it when we were not there."

"Tomorrow I'll go to the garage and call on our cell phone to make arrangements."

"Okay. How are you going to get me to the lodge without someone following us?"

I thought for a minute, then an idea came to me.

"I'm going to have us arrested?"

"Arrested?"

"Well, not really. I'm going to have us picked up by the police. We'll pack some clothes in cardboard boxes. Then I'll get Gerrie Baker to come with a couple of uniformed patrol officers to pick us up. They will make it look like we are under arrest. The boxes will look like evidence might be in them."

"When are we going to pull off this little charade?"

"Tomorrow morning, if I can get it arranged. I doubt I will be able to get hold of Gerrie tonight. Right now, we are going back to the apartment and get some sleep."

"Do you think I can get any sleep knowing that someone might be listening in on everything we say?"

"Probably not, but we have to make everything we say sound as normal as possible."

"Okay."

Monica and I returned to our apartment then went to bed. She snuggled up to me and I held her in my arms. We were both very tired. We had been working hard in our effort to find out who had done what to whom. We had two deaths to investigate, and the threats on our person. They were all connected in some way, but I still wasn't sure how.

What did Ricker know that he didn't get the chance to tell us? What part did he play in this, if he had any part in it at all? Was he just a guy who found something on the track? He may have been, but how did he know that the partial bolts with nuts on them might be important to what happened? And what did he know about the small piece of metal he found, and what did it have to do with anything?

So many questions were running through my mind that it was hard to shut down my brain to get some sleep. I was glad to see that with Monica in my arms, she felt safe enough to go to sleep. It took me a long time to get to sleep. I woke up often to check on her, and each time she was snuggled up against me.

Morning came early. I had fallen asleep and woke up thinking about what today would bring. I needed to make two phone calls. One to Tom Walker at his lodge out at Gill's Point, and one to Lieutenant Gerrie Baker.

"What are you thinking about?" Monica asked.

"About what I have to do this morning."

"Are you ready to get up?"

"Yes. I'll get breakfast started," I said.

She smiled as I got out of bed. As soon as I was dressed, I went to the kitchen and began fixing breakfast. It wasn't long before Monica came into the kitchen. She sat down while I put breakfast on the table, then I sat across from her. Before she could speak, I reminded her that the place might be bugged. I moved close to her so she could whisper in my ear.

"Have you decided how you're going to get us out of here without anyone knowing we have left?" she whispered.

"Yes, but we are leaving here so anyone who might be watching will know we left."

Monica smiled then whispered, "I have always known you were sneaky."

We didn't talk any more. After breakfast, I went to the garage and used my cell phone to place a call to Gill's Point lodge.

"Gill's Point Lodge, how may I help you?" Tom asked.

"You can put Monica up for a few days," I said.

"Nick, is that you?"

"Yes. I need a favor."

"Sure. Anything."

"I need you to put Monica up at the lodge under a fictious name."

"Sure, no problem. Is she in some sort of danger?"

"It's possible. While she is there, she will be doing research for me while I follow up leads on a case we are working on here."

"I see. You know you are always welcome here. I'll reserve a room for her where she can work undisturbed."

"Thanks."

"When can I expect her?"

"It will probably be late this afternoon or early tonight."

"Will you be coming with her?"

"Probably not, but I'm not sure yet."

"Okay, I'll be ready for her. What name will she be using?"

"Wilma van Hunt from Vancouver, British Columbia."

"Why so far away?"

"It will make it harder to trace her background if she is from Canada."

"Okay, I'll make a reservation for her in that name."

"Thanks. I'll talk to you later.

"Okay. Be careful out there."

"I will," I said then hung up.

Monica joined me just as I finished my phone call to Tom. I took a minute to tell Monica that she had a reservation at Gill's Point Lodge. She chuckled a bit when I told her the name she was registered under.

I then placed a call to Lieutenant Gerrie Baker. I told her of my plan to get out of the area. I also told her that our apartment might be bugged and she should treat us as if we were really being arrested. She agreed with it and told me she would be by in about an hour.

Monica and I returned to our apartment and began gathering up all the files and information we had put together on all our suspects along with any evidence we had and placed it in a couple of cardboard boxes. Monica put a small suit case together and put it in a box.

We were ready to put our plan into action as soon as Lieutenant Baker showed up. We sat down to wait. Monica leaned up against me. We didn't talk, we just sat close together.

CHAPTER FIFTEEN

It wasn't very long before we heard a police car come roaring into the parking lot, without sirens. I got up from the sofa and walked to the window. A patrol car with flashing lights pulled to a stop in front of our apartment building. I noticed a dark colored sedan with a flashing red light on the dash following it.

"I wonder what's going on," I said.

If nothing else Gerrie put on a show for whoever might be watching or listening. The two officers from the patrol car came running up the stairs. Suddenly, there was some hard knocking on the door to our apartment.

"Open up. This is the police," an officer yelled out.

I looked at Monica and smiled as I walked to the door. I opened the door. The two officers pushed their way into our apartment."

"You are under arrest," the sergeant said.

Gerrie walked into the apartment behind the officers. I signaled that the place might be bugged as a reminder of what I told her when I made arrangements for this little play. She nodded that she remembered.

"Nick McCord, you are under arrest for the murder of Billy Ricker of Calumet City, Illinois. And Monica McCord, you are under arrest as an accomplice," Gerrie said with a strong tone of authority.

I handed the cardboard boxes to the younger officer. The sergeant handcuffed us as Gerrie read us our rights.

"Take them away," Gerrie said.

We were taken out and put in the patrol car along with the two cardboard boxes. After a couple of more boxes were filled, Gerrie walked out of the apartment and locked the door. She took the boxes and put them in her car. We were taken to the police station where the handcuffs were removed. We sat down in front of Gerrie's desk.

"I hope I never really get arrested by you. I don't like the feel of handcuffs," I said.

"You said you wanted it to look real, real you got." Gerrie replied with a grin. "By the way, we have put 'Crime Scene' yellow tape across your door to make it look real. We are also having a plain clothes officer watching your apartment to see if anyone tries to get in."

"The 'Crime Scene" tape was a nice touch. Now all we have to do is get Monica to Gill's Point without anyone knowing."

"I've got a trusted officer who will drive her up to Gill's Point in his own car with whatever she needs. He will be in plain clothes and will help her get her computer set up once they are in the lodge. Monica can brief him on the way.

"I have a couple of detectives who are on their way to your apartment to remove your computers, as evidence of course, and bring them here. We'll put them in the car in the police garage.

"Once that is done, Monica will get in the car and lay down in the backseat. She will be taken to the lodge at Gill's Point. The officer is doing this on his own time as a favor to me. By the way, he knows you from the class you taught on preserving evidence. Apparently, he thinks highly of you."

"I appreciate that. Don't worry. I will see to it he gets paid well for his time, mileage, and for any help he is to her."

"I hoped you would compensate him. When you walk out of here without Monica, how do you plan to keep whoever is threatening you from knowing that Monica has been hidden away?"

"Once she is safe and out of harm's way, I don't think it will matter. They will have to focus on me, but I will be hard to find. I don't plan to leave here until she is safe in Gill's Point Lodge. I plan to sneak out of here as well. I'll leave here in one of the patrols cars when it leaves to go on its routine patrol this evening. I'll have them drop me off some place where I can get a room."

I turned and looked when an officer in civilian clothes stuck his head in the door.

"We're ready. We have the computers in the car. Everything is ready to go."

"Thanks," Gerrie said.

"It's time for you to leave," Gerrie said.

"Thank you for your help," Monica said.

"You're welcome."

I walked with Monica down the back way to the police garage which was attached to the police station. I had the two cardboard boxes with me. When we got to the car that was to take her to Gill's Point, I put the boxes in the trunk. I noticed her computer, and everything she would need was already in the trunk. I closed the trunk, then opened the backdoor of the car.

Monica stepped up in front of me and put her arms around my neck. I wrapped my arms around her and pulled her close to me. We kissed. I leaned back and looked at her.

"I'll call you this evening. When you get to your room, get set up and start going through the reports we have, and get reports on the ones we don't. I'm hoping you will be able to find some clues to who and what is going on."

"I will try my best."

"I'm sure you will. I love you."

"I love you. Be careful."

"I will," I said then I kissed her again. "You best get going."

Monica looked at me then turned and got in the backseat of the car. As I closed the backdoor, Monica glanced up at me for a second then laid down on the seat.

The officer, dressed in civilian clothes, had gotten in what appeared to be his own car and was waiting for us. As soon as the backdoor closed, the officer started the car and drove out of the police garage.

I stood by and watched as the car left the garage. There was little question in my mind that this investigation could get nasty. At least, Monica would be safe, leaving me free to find the truth without the need to worry about her safety.

As soon as the car was out of sight, I turned around and went back inside the station. I returned to Gerrie's office.

"I take it she is on her way."

"Yes. It will take them a couple of hours to get to the lodge. I hope he is keeping an eye out for anyone who might be following them."

"I'm sure he is. I told him to be careful and watch for anyone who might be following them. He is not to take her to the lodge if he suspects they are being followed."

"Good."

"I guess it is time to wait."

"I guess so. Where do you want me to wait?" I asked.

"You can wait here in my office. What do you have so far? Anything that should concern me here in Madison?"

"Most of my suspects are from Illinois."

"I have CSI going to your apartment to see if it is bugged."

"Thanks. I'm not sure it is bugged, but I didn't want to take the chance."

"We'll find out if it is," Gerrie said.

"By the way, did you get the criminal record on Stoker?"

"Yes. I have it right here."

"May I see it now."

"Sure."

Gerrie handed me the file containing the criminal record from the Chicago, Illinois, Police Department. It had CONFIDENCIAL in big red letters written on the front of the file.

"You can use the table over there, if you like," she said as she pointed at the table.

"Thank you."

I moved over to the table and sat down. After opening the file, I began looking at the contents. I examined each page for anything of interest. No person I have ever known had so many arrests as Stoker, and had not served more than one night in jail. It looked like in most cases he had been bailed out within a few hours of his arrest.

It was hard to understand how he was so well known and respected in his community with so many arrests. I had to think that he managed to keep that information out of the newspapers and news broadcasts.

For the average person, it would be almost impossible to keep their record of arrests out of the newspapers. He had to have some very good connections in Chicago.

I remembered being told that he had a lot of influence with judges and attorneys. There was little doubt in my mind that he might also have some influence with the local newspapers as well. I wondered what it cost to have so much influence, especially with judges and attorneys.

In among the papers in the file, I also noticed that there were several names that I didn't recognizes. I wondered who they were and what connection they had to Stoker.

"Gerrie, who are these people."

Gerrie came over and looked over my shoulder. I pointed to the names.

"Those are Stoker's muscles. I didn't ask for their files."

"That's okay. I may want them later, but for now I will focus on Stoker."

I studied the names. It wasn't until I turned the page that I found one I recognized. It was Josh Ellis, Barbara's Personal Assistant.

"Well, well. So that's who you really work for," I said out load to myself.

"Did you find something?"

"I sure did. The muscle named Josh Ellis. I met him at the Smith estate. He introduced himself as Barbara Smith's

Personal Assistant. This gives me a lot to think about. He may be the reason that Barbara changed her comment about the death of her husband."

"What do you mean?"

"She called me the night that Brandon died in the crash and almost yelled at me that it was murder. But when I saw her at the Smith estate a few days later, she referred to it as an accident. It would be my guess that Ellis is there to keep her under control."

Gerrie looked at the paper with his name on it. She then looked at me.

"I'd be darn careful around him. He has been arrested several times for assault with intent to do bodily harm in the Chicago area. As I recall, he was arrested here in Madison for almost killing a man with his bare hands for accidently bumping into him in a crowded bar near the ballpark. The man was so frightened of him that he refused to press charges. We had to turn him loose because the man refused to file a complaint, and there were no witnesses, at least none that would come forward."

"It would be my guess that several of these others would be just as violent."

"Maybe, but Ellis is certifiably crazy. Once he is in a fight, he goes for the kill. The only reason he didn't kill the man was the cops got there and subdued him with a tazer. He was arrested for resisting arrest by the officers."

As soon as Gerrie returned to her desk, I returned to the file on Stoker. I made a few notes. There were a few things that I wanted Monica to look up for me.

I became so engrossed in the file on Stoker and the names of his henchmen that I lost all track of time. Gerrie walked over to the table where I was working.

"Nick, I'm going to get something to eat. Would you like something."

"Ah – yeah. But I don't think I should go outside or walk around in here where someone might see me."

"I was thinking of getting something from the lounge here in the station. It's vending machine food, but it fills the stomach. Would you like me to get you a sandwich and a drink?"

"Yes. A ham and cheese sandwich, if there is one. Anything will do. A Coke would be fine."

"I'll be right back."

It wasn't long before Gerrie returned to her office with a couple of sandwiches and drinks. She gave me what I asked for, then sat down at her desk. I turned my chair around and sat down in front of her desk. We talked while we ate.

"How are things going?"

"Not bad. This fella, Stoker, is a real piece of work. He has quite a setup. He's a well-known and well-respected businessman, a golfer and member of a prestigious country club, antique car owner and an officer in a fancy antique car club; and he's a church going man who gives generously to his church.

"Yet, at the same time, he is as ruthless a mobster as you can get. He actually lives two separate and completely different lives, and nobody even knows, or seems to care."

"That's all the more reason you have to be careful around him. You try to put a dent in his well-planned workings, and he'll kill you without giving it a second thought. And he will probably get away with it."

I looked at Gerrie for a moment. I was sure that her comment was true. I was also sure that it was a warning to me to be very careful when talking to or even searching for information on Stoker, his friends and employees, or his family. There was little doubt in my mind that I would be very careful.

Time passed rather slowly. It was almost two-thirty in the afternoon when I got the call from Monica that she was safe in Gill's Point Lodge. She had registered as Wilma van Hunt. I would call her that as long as she was there, just in case someone would inquire about Monica.

I got a chance to talk to her for a few minutes. Most of our conversation was about the investigation and what I needed her to do. I told her that I would call her about two in the afternoon, tomorrow. We reluctantly ended the call after only a few minutes. I explained that I needed to find a place to hide out for a day or so while looking into our suspects.

I found it hard to hang up, but I needed to find out who threatened us and get him out of the picture.

I spent the next couple of hours digging through the information in the file on Stoker. The deeper I got into it, the more I began to understand the man. I also got a feel for the attorneys he had working for him, and why they were so loyal to him. My best guess was part of the reason for their loyalty was just plain fear.

CHAPTER SIXTEEN

It was time for the evening shift of patrolmen to go on duty. Gerrie arranged for the patrolmen in one of the patrol cars to sneak me out of the police station and take me to a motel. I got in the backseat of the patrol car. One of the officers looked over his shoulder at me.

"Where would you like to go, Mr. McCord?"

"I don't want to be any more of a bother than necessary. What is the nearest motel with a place to get something to eat close by in your patrol area?"

"There's a Motel 6 with a restaurant right next door."

"That would be fine."

"Okay. You best lay down on the seat. Lieutenant Baker said we are to get you out of here without anyone seeing you leave."

"Right."

I laid down on the backseat. I could tell when the car left the building. It wasn't very long before the officer driving spoke.

"We're about ten blocks from the station. We haven't seen anyone following us. I think you can sit up."

"Thanks," I said as I sat up and looked around. "When you get close to the motel, drop me off about a block or so from it."

"Okay."

I watched for anyone following us, but didn't see anyone. It was only about ten minutes before the officer driving the patrol car pulled over to the curb and stopped. He turned in his seat and looked back at me.

"I don't see anyone around. The motel is around the corner and about a block down the street to the right. We'll follow you until you get in the office."

"That would be great. How about I buy you dinner for your troubles?"

"We can't take it. We're on duty. If we were doing this on our own time, in our own car, and out of uniform, we could except it."

"I understand," I said.

I got out of the car and looked around. I didn't see anyone. I leaned down and looked into the patrol car.

"Thanks, guys. I owe you each a lunch sometime when our paths cross again. Thanks again."

"You don't owe us anything. Good luck, Mr. McCord," the officer driving said.

I stepped away from the car and began to walk to the corner. I turned right and walked down the block to the Motel 6. When I turned to go into the office of the motel, I glanced back. I could see the patrol car still at the corner. They had been watching me. I was glad to know they took their job seriously. I gave them a slight nod of my head and they drove around the corner and passed me.

I turned and walked into the office of the motel. There were two people in the office, a young lady at the counter and a middle-aged man sitting at a desk behind a partition. The young lady looked up and smiled.

"May I help you," she asked.

"I would like a room for the night."

"Would that be for one?"

"Yes, and for one night. It doesn't need to be anything fancy, just quiet."

"All our rooms are pretty much the same. I'll put you in a room toward the back, away from the traffic."

"That would be fine."

I took my wallet out and handed her my credit card. She looked at it, then ran it through her machine. Within a couple of seconds, she printed me a receipt. I signed it than filled out a registration card. She handed me a key to the room.

During the process of registering for the room, I noticed the man behind the partition was watching me. I was sure he was the manager. He was probably curious why I had walked in to get a room and didn't have any luggage. I decided to call down to the office as soon as I got to my room.

I walked down the hall to my room. I looked around as I put the key in the door. I didn't see anyone, then entered the room.

After closing the door and securing it, I looked around the room. It wasn't anything fancy, but it was nice, and more important, it was clean.

I sat down on the bed, picked up the phone and called the office. The phone rang only twice before it was answered by a man.

"This is the manager, may I help you?"

"Yes. Would you be so kind as to come to my room? I would like to talk to you."

"I'll be right there, sir," then the phone went dead.

It wasn't but about three minutes when there was a knock on the door. I peeked out the peep hole in the door and saw it was the manager. I carefully opened the door, then let him in. Once he was in the room, I quickly checked to see if there was anyone one else around. It was clear. I closed the door.

"I noticed you were watching me rather carefully when I checked in."

"I have to admit, I was curious since you did not come in a car, and you did not have any luggage."

"I'm sure you have had others come in without luggage, and you probably didn't see a car. Am I right?"

"Well, . . . yes, sir."

"Then, why the interest in me?"

"The way you are dressed would make me think that you would have had luggage and most likely a car."

"In other words, I look like the type who would get a motel room and then sneak a woman in later."

"Yes, sir. I mean, no, sir."

"For your information, why I'm at your motel is none of your business unless I plan to do something illegal or against your motel's rules. I am not here to do anything illegal or against company polices. Is that clear?"

"Yes, sir."

"If you wish to keep your job as manager, I suggest you say nothing about my being here to anyone. My reasons are legal and above board, but none of your business. Do you understand? Not a word to anyone that I even exist."

"Yes, sir."

"Good. I will be calling for a cab in the morning, and you will forget you ever saw me," I said.

I quickly flashed my PI badge so he could only get a glimpse of it. From the look on his face, I was sure he thought I was a law enforcement officer."

"Yes, sir. I won't say a word to anyone."

"Thank you. You may go now."

"Thank you, sir."

I watched as he left the room. Under any other circumstances I might have grinned, but I needed him to keep quiet. I didn't want anyone to know where I was, or why I was here. As I thought about it, I was sure that it was a wise decision for me to have already planned to spend just one night there.

I took a few minutes to watch a little television before I took a shower. It was then that I realized that I didn't have anything clean to wear. I had been so concerned with making sure Monica had what she needed and was safe, I forgot to get clothes and a shaving kit for myself.

It had been a long day with a lot of emotions. I missed Monica, and wished I could be with her at Gill's Point Lodge. I had fond memories of that place. It was where I met Monica, although the circumstances had been less than ideal.

It took me awhile to get to sleep. I knew tomorrow was going to be a busy day for me. I had several things to do, and several people to check on. I finally drifted off to sleep.

When morning came, I dressed in the same clothes I had on yesterday. I thought about going back to the apartment to get a few things, but didn't want to take the chance of being seen there. That being the case, I decided to check out of the motel, get a cab and go to a mall to get some clothes.

I also needed a set of wheels. To go back to the apartment to get my car was probably not a good idea. It was a good possibility that my car was being watched in case I was released from custody. It would also be easily recognized by those interested in finding me if seen on the street.

I called for a cab. When it arrived, I had the cabby take me to a mall. I went into Penney's and bought two sets of clothes and a few other things I would need. One of them being a small suitcase to put them in. I changed into the new clothes in the fitting room. Then I went to a drug store in the mall to get what toiletries I would need.

Once I had what I needed, and had them in the suitcase, I called for a cab. I took the cab to a Ford dealership. I was met by one of the hotshot salesmen. I cut him off from his usual sales pitch and told him what I wanted. He actually seemed relieved.

"I have several Explorers, sir. Do you have a color preference?"

"No, but I do have a few options I would like."

I told him what I wanted for options. He looked it up, then told me he had four Explorers that had the options I wanted, one was blue, one was red and two were white. White Explorers seemed to be very popular, at least I had seen a lot of them on the road, which might not be a bad thing for me. I told him I would take one of the white ones, but I wanted it ready to drive as quickly as possible.

We sat down and dickered over the price. With the fact that I had no trade-in, and I was paying cash up front, I was able to get a good price. I called my banker, explained what I wanted to do. He made the necessary arrangements for the money to be sent to the dealership, and I filled out the necessary paperwork.

As soon as the money was transferred to the dealership, the salesman had the Explorer made ready. It was ready to go in just short of an hour. During that time, I arranged for insurance on the vehicle through my insurance agent. Within an hour and a half, I was driving down the road headed for Calumet City, Illinois in my new Explorer.

As I drove toward Calumet City, I began to think about what had taken place there. I quickly realized that I had no plan. My first thought was to find Neil Upton and confront him with his call to me and the threats he used over the phone. The one thing I was sure of was he had been forced to make the calls. The questions I had were who made Upton make the calls, and what did that person have on Upton that he was holding over his head?

I also wanted to know what was going on with the company that Brandon had built. Why was it being sold off to a guy like Stoker? Did Brandon even know it was being sold off? I had to think that Brandon might have been killed because he either, found out that his company was being sold off right under his nose, or he suspected it was being sold off, but didn't have time before the race to confirm his suspicions.

Then came the question, who would be able to sell off the company without him knowing? The answer to that question was rather simple. The person who could sell off the business without Brandon knowing would probably be the person who handled the business affairs, his wife, and or his business attorney, George Moorhouse.

I got the impression from my first visit to the Smith Estate that his wife handled the business side of the company. George Moorhouse was probably helping her sell it off to Stoker, since she had commented on Moorhouse being her business adviser. However, if George Moorhouse had a Power of Attorney to handle her business affairs, he could probably sell off the business without her knowing.

Something else came to mind. The building I saw Brandon's Ferrari in was not being used. I was told a new building was being readied with new equipment, and the old equipment was to be sold off. It might be wise for me to find out who really owned the new building. If I had to guess, the first name that came to mind was William F. Stoker. Then came the question, was there a new building?

With all the different thoughts racing through my mind, the one person who might know the answers to some of them was Russell Larson. He was the only one who seemed to be really concerned with finding out if Brandon's death was an accident or murder. I was also sure that he would be under a lot of pressure to keep quiet.

It was becoming clearer that I needed to talk to Russell. He was the one person who I might be able to get to talk to me if I could get him alone without anyone knowing.

The best place to find him alone would be at the old plant. The problem was how was I going to get into the old plant without the guard at the gate knowing I was there? My new vehicle would not be known by the guard as it was not the same vehicle we had when Monica and I visited the plant. It was time to head for the old plant and drive by to see if it was still being watched, and to get some idea how difficult it would be to get into it.

I arrived at the road that went by the front of the old plant shortly before four o'clock in the afternoon. I turned onto the road and drove by the plant without making it look like I was showing any interest in the building.

There was a single car in the parking lot. It was parked close to the walk-in door next to the large overhead door. I didn't see a vehicle near the guardhouse like the last time I was there.

As I drove past the entrance to the plant, I didn't see a guard in the guardhouse. It occurred to me that maybe the plant was now empty so a guard was not needed. I also noticed that the gate was not completely closed. As I continued on down the road, it occurred to me that I could easily drive in and go to the building.

When I got to the crossroad at the end of the plant's property, I turned around and stopped. I sat there looking at the plant and wondering what I might find if I drove through the gate and went up to the building.

I stared at the car parked in front of the building. The car was nothing special, but I couldn't help but think that I had seen it before. It suddenly came to me. The car was Russell's. I asked myself, "What was he doing here if the plant was empty?". Everything pointed to the plant being empty except for Russell's car parked out in front.

It was at that moment, I decided that I would take the chance that Russell was inside the building, alone. I drove up to the gate, stopped, and got out of my vehicle and checked to see if there was anyone in the guardhouse or on the property. I saw no one. I pushed open the gate, then returned to my vehicle. I got in and drove up to the building, parking next to Russell's car.

As I got out of my vehicle, I looked around, but didn't see anyone. I walked up to the walk-in door, reached out and turned the doorknob. The door was unlocked and opened easily.

Being as cautious as possible, I looked inside, then stepped into the plant closing the door behind me. I moved to the side of the door away from the window. I stood close to the door while I looked around and listened. There was not a sound. It was as if I had stepped into a tomb.

From where I was standing, I could see the white paint booth. The door was open, and I could only see the rear of the wrecked Ferrari. It was still in the paint booth on the trailer. However, there were no lights on inside the paint booth.

It struck me as strange that the paint booth was open. The last time I had seen the paint booth was when Russell locked it after my inspection of the car.

I turned and looked at the office. The first thing I noticed was all the office furniture and files had been removed. My first thought was it seemed logical since I was told they were moving to a new building. One look around the plant from next to the office, I could see that the large machines were still there. I began to realize that nothing in the plant had change in the past week, except the office had been emptied. Almost everything else was just the way I had seen it when I left there after examining the car, except the door to the paint booth was open.

I had a strange feeling come over me. My first thought was to get out of the plant as quickly as possible. It almost felt like it was a trap, and I had walked right into it.

At that moment, I remembered that Russell's car was out front. Where was Russell? It occurred to me that Russell was probably somewhere in this plant. I decided to take a quick look in the paint booth before I left. It was the only thing in the plant that was different, except the office furniture being removed.

I walked over to the paint booth. From the door, I could not see very much. Even though the door was open, there was little light inside the paint booth. The only light was from outside the booth. I got a funny feeling that something was wrong.

I walked into the paint booth and slowly started to walk around the car. When I got to the front of the booth, I found Russell. He was lying on the floor. I knelt down, but with so little light, I couldn't see if he was injured.

I reached out to touch his neck to see if he was alive, but was disturbed by the sound of the door closing. I quickly stood up and turned toward the door, but didn't have time to get to the door before it closed completely. I could hear the sound of someone outside the paint booth locking the door.

I quickly realized that I had walked right into a trap. My problem was that I didn't know how I was going to get out.

CHAPTER SEVENTEEN

I had suddenly found myself in almost total darkness. I reached over by the door and ran my hand along the wall in the hope of finding a light switch to turn on the lights. I didn't find one. It was at that moment I remembered that the light switch was on the outside of the paint booth.

All of sudden the lights in the paint booth came on. Looking around, it became clear that there was no other way out of the paint booth than through the door.

I walked to the front of the Ferrari to check on Russell. The first thing I noticed was his head had been smashed in. There was a rather large and very heavy wrench lying right beside him, and it was covered with blood. There was no need to check to see if he was alive. It was obvious that the wrench had been used to kill him.

I quickly realized that with all the lights on inside the paint booth, it was going to get very hot in a very short time. I needed to do something and do it quickly. Breaking the lights seemed like the logical thing to do, since there was no light switch inside the paint booth.

On the other hand, I needed at least a few lights left on or I would be in total darkness, again. The only solution was to break most of the light bulbs to reduce the heat.

I began breaking the lights until I only had two lights that still worked, but they gave off enough light to see inside the paint booth without producing much heat. Breaking the light bulbs only gave me more time to figure out what to do.

I looked around to see if I could find something that I could use to pry the door open. The only tool I could find was the wrench I was sure had been used to kill Russell. I didn't want to touch it. There might be fingerprints on it, though I doubted there would be any. I also doubted that it would be much help in prying the door open since it didn't have any sharp edges that I could slip in the edge of the door to pry it open.

I checked my cell phone to see if I could get a signal inside the paint booth. No luck. It had no signal.

I began looking over the inside of the paint booth. If I remembered correctly there was a vent of some kind that drew the fumes from the paint out of the paint booth while whatever was in the booth was being painted. I began looking for the vent. I discovered it up close to the top of the booth on the back wall. The grill on the front of the vent didn't look like it was very strong. My problem was would I be able to pull the grill off, and if I did, what would I find behind it.

The first problem was how was I going to get up there to pull the grill off. The vent was above my head where I could barely reach the bottom of the vent cover. Trying to pull it off from over my head gave me very little leverage. Looking around, I noticed the paint bench had casters on it. It would not normally be in the booth while the booth was used to dry the paint on the item that had been painted, but it had apparently been stored in the booth when not in use.

I rolled the paint bench over to the wall just below the vent. I climbed up on it. I gripped the grill on the vent and gave it a hard jerk. It came off much easier than I had expected. I almost lost my balance and fell off the bench.

Once I got the filters out of the way, I was able to break the vent ducks away from the booth. The hole left was too small for me to climb out, but I was able to get a signal on my cell phone by holding it outside the booth. I placed a call to Joe Martin. It didn't take long before he answered the phone.

"Detective Martin, how may I help you."

"Joe, this is Nick. I need you to come and get me."

"Where are you?"

"I'm in the paint booth in Smith's plant, the old plant where the Ferrari is located."

"You're in the paint booth? What the hell are you doing there?"

I could hear a slight chuckle in his voice.

"I'll explain later, but you might want to bring along a forensic team, and something to cut the lock off the door. It seems that Russell Larson is also locked in here with me, only he's dead. He was murdered."

"I'm on my way," he said then the phone went dead.

All I could do now was wait and think about who wanted me dead. Right off the top of my head, I could think of several people who might like to see me dead. Ellis and Stoker were the first two names that came to mind.

While I was waiting, I walked around the Ferrari. I couldn't help but think that this car had something to do with Brandon's death, besides being the car that had crashed at the racetrack. It had been used as the weapon that killed him. It didn't seem like a very reliable way to kill someone. Something had to have been done to it to make sure it would crash. It required another look at it, but that would have to wait until I could get it in better lighting.

I don't know how long I waited for Joe to get to the plant, but it wasn't very long before I heard someone banging on the door. Suddenly the door opened. Joe was standing there looking at me.

"You all right?"

"Yeah. Russell is in front of the car."

I stepped out of the paint booth and then stood there while Joe walked around to the front of the car. I thought I could hear him gasp when he saw the body. It was not a pretty sight. It was only a minute or so when I saw him stand up and look at me over the car.

"Is this Russell Larson?"

"It is."

"What can you tell me about him?" Joe asked as he walked toward me.

"He was Brandon Smith's mechanic. He was also the one who called me and told me that he thought Brandon had been murdered. He wanted me to look at the car to see if I could prove the car had been tampered with so it would crash. He thought that the car had been tampered with causing it to crash."

"The parts we found at Ricker's place came from this car?"

"We are pretty sure the bolts you found at Ricker's came from this car, but the piece of metal, we don't know. I have not received the reports on the bolts and piece of metal from the lab examining them. I will get a copy of the report to you as soon as I get one."

"Okay."

Joe turned and looked at the car. It was clear that he was thinking. After a minute or so, he turned and looked at me again.

"Nick, do you have any idea who might have locked you in the paint booth?"

"No. I was kneeling down looking at Russell when I heard the door close. When I stood up so I could see over the car, the door was already closed. By the time I could get to the door, it had been locked. Besides, I didn't want to go charging out of the paint booth. That could have been fatal."

"I'm sure. I'm going to have some explaining to do with the Chief. This is the second body you've found in less than three days."

"I hope I'm not causing you problems."

"No, I don't think so. I can probably explain it to him," Joe said.

"I have a question for you. Did you see Russell's car out in front?"

"The only vehicle out in front of the building is a new white Explorer. Since you are the only one I've seen, besides Russell, and the Explorer has Wisconsin temporary plates on it, I assume it is your vehicle."

"Yes, it is my Explorer. But when I came in here, Russell's car was parked next to mine."

"Are you sure his car was parked out in front?"

"Yes. It was parked right next to mine. And I'm sure it was Russell's car because I have seen it before."

"When was that?"

"When I first came to inspect the Ferrari at Russell's and Mrs. Smith's request."

"I wonder where it is now?" Joe said.

"I would like to know, too. It might be a good idea to put an APB out on the car. If you find it, have your forensic people go over."

"I will. By the way, how did all the lights in the paint booth get broken?

"I did that. It would have gotten very hot in there if I had left all the lights on."

"I'm sure it would. Do you think that whoever locked you in the paint booth expected you do die in there?"

"It crossed my mind, but I didn't have much time to think about it. You just might be right. There wouldn't be anyone around here for, I don't know how long. A couple of days in this place with the hot lights would have probably killed me."

"I think we need to assume that whoever locked you in, intended to kill you."

"I already think that, and I plan to find out who it was," I said.

"What are your plans now?"

"I think a visit to Mrs. Barbara Smith is in order."

"You think she had you locked in the paint booth? How would she know you were here?"

"I doubt that she knows anything about it. I wouldn't put it past Josh Ellis to be the one to kill Russell and lock me in the paint booth."

"How would he know you were here?"

"I don't think he did. I think he got Russell to come out here to the plant using some made up excuse. Once he got Russell here, he killed him. His plan was probably to drive Russell's car away so no one would think anyone was here. My arrival interrupted his plan. I showed up before he could get out of here, so he had to deal with me."

"That sounds reasonable," Joe said.

"I also don't think Ellis would have killed Russell without orders from his boss."

"Isn't Barbara Smith his boss? I know he works for her."

"She may think he works for her, but I'd be willing to bet he really works for someone else. I'm just not sure who that someone else is."

"If we assume the killer was here when you got here, and Russell's car was the only one here, how did the killer get here if Russell's car was the only car here when you got here?"

"That's a good question. My guess would be he either came here with Russell on some made up pretense, then drove away in Russell's car after he killed Russell and locked me in the paint booth. Possibly, someone else brought him here then left. My best guess is he came here with Russell."

"You're saying that he came here with Russell, killed Russell, then drove off with his car."

"Right."

"Why would he do that?"

"So, Russell's car would not be parked out in front of the plant to draw attention," I said.

Joe looked from me to the paint booth. I was sure he was thinking about what I had said. After a minute or so he turned back and looked at me.

"I think the Ferrari should be taken to our forensic lab and have them go over every inch of that car. I'll also have them go over this paint booth."

"I think that is a good idea. Would you let me know what you find?"

"Sure. What's you next move, Nick?"

"I think I'll pay a visit to Mrs. Barbara Smith. I want to see the look on her face when I show up at her estate."

"Nick, I want you to stay in touch with me. Someone is out to get you off this case."

"I'm sure you're right. I'll keep in touch."

Joe nodded then walked out of the plant. I followed him out of the plant and went directly to my vehicle. I noticed he talked to one of the officers who had showed up at the same time he arrived. From the looks of things, he told the officer to secure the building, and wait for the forensic team to show up. I watched as he went to his car, sat down, and began talking on his police radio. There was little doubt in my mind that he was calling in for a forensic team, and putting out an APB for Russell's car. There was nothing else I could do here, so I started my vehicle and drove away.

It didn't take me very long to get to the front gate of the Smith estate. When I pulled to a stop at the gate, I noticed the guard was not Neil Upton. My guess was he either was off duty, or he was at the back gate where I first met him. I stopped next to the guardhouse. The young man at the gate, looked at me for a second or so before he approached my vehicle.

"Can I help you, sir?"

"I would like to speak to Mrs. Smith.

"Your name, sir?"

"Nick McCord."

"Just a minute."

The guard stepped back in the guardhouse and phoned the house. I could see him, but could not hear him. I could see him mouth the words, "Yes, Ma'am."

He hung up the phone, then turned to me. I couldn't tell by the look on his face if he was going to let me in or not.

"Mrs. Smith is not in at the moment. Her personal assistant suggested you call for an appointment."

There was little doubt that he was lying to me. I knew her personal assistant was a man. I looked up at the house as I thought about what my next move would be, when the guard interrupted my thoughts.

"Do you wish to make an appointment, sir?"

"Ah – no. I'll call later to make an appointment."

"Yes, sir."

The guard stepped back away from my vehicle. I backed up and turned around. As I drove back to the street. I could see the guard was still watching me.

I headed for a place where I could get a room. I found a small motel that would allow me to park my vehicle off the street and out of sight from the street. I pulled in and went directly to the motel office. As soon as I had registered and gotten a key to the room, I moved my vehicle so it could not be seen from the street, then went to my room.

Once I was in the room, I sat down at the desk and placed a call to Wilma van Hunt, aka Monica. It didn't take her but a couple of seconds to answer her phone.

"How are you?'

"I'm fine. I miss you," I said.

"I miss you, too. How is it going?"

"Not very well. I had to buy a new vehicle. I got a new Explorer."

"Oh. How come?"

I could hear in her voice that she was worried. She probably thought the worst.

I explained that my car was probably being watched. I didn't want to be seen by going to get it. A new car was one way to avoid going to our apartment to get it. She grasped the situation right away.

"That was probably a good idea. Is everything else going okay?" Monica asked.

"Not really. I went to the plant to meet with Russell. When I got there, I found him dead in front of the Ferrari in the paint booth."

"Oh, – I guess that takes care of one of our suspects."

"It sure does."

"Where are you now?"

"I'm in Calumet City, in a small motel off the beaten path."

"Good. Any idea why Russell was killed?"

"My best guess would be to make sure he didn't talk. About what, I don't know. I suspect he found something that someone didn't want him to find.

"Joe is taking the Ferrari to the police lab to have the forensic people look it over every inch of it. I have no idea what he might find, but at least it is out of the hands of anyone who could ruin any evidence it might still have."

"That's good. You sound tired."

"I am. I stopped by the Smith Estate. I wanted to talk to Barbara, but the guard at the gate wouldn't let me in. He said she was not available and that I should call for an appointment. I know she was there from the actions of the guard."

"What are you going to do?" Monica asked.

"I think I'm going to find Moorhouse and shake him up a little."

"You be careful around him."

"I will. Have you found anything new?"

"I think so. Do you know that Stoker was arrested for punching a vintage car owner in the face? The vintage car owner beat him out of first place at a car show in Arizona two years ago? Stoker was suspended from showing his cars at any car show in Arizona for two years and fined eight thousand dollars," Monica said.

"No, I didn't know that. However, it answers two questions for me. Those being, he has a temper and he is a poor loser. If he punched out a guy who beat him once, what would he do to someone who beat him four out of five times, with three of those times in a row?"

"He would probably kill him."

"Right. That supports one of our motives."

"It sure does.

"I doubt it will get him arrested, however," I said.

"You're probably right."

We spent the next few minutes just talking, mostly how much we missed each other. It was getting late and I had had a full day. I finally said goodnight and hung up after a few kisses over the phone.

Once I finished my call to Monica, I took a shower then laid down on the bed. I turned on the local news just in time to hear about a body being found in a deserted plant on the outskirts of Calumet City. There was very little information. The name of the victim was not mentioned, nor was the cause of death. I doubted the police would release the victim's name, or the cause of death, at least for a while.

I decided to turn off the television and get some rest. Since things were getting a little nasty, I put my gun under my pillow, then laid down to get some rest. It wasn't long before I was sound asleep.

CHAPTER EIGHTEEN

I woke early and immediately got dressed. Once I was dressed and had my things packed up, I took a minute to look outside. I saw two men walking toward the office. As soon as they were in the office, I slipped out and put my luggage in the backseat of my Explorer, then slid into the driver seat. I started it and quickly left the parking lot.

As I pulled out onto the street, I glanced over toward the office of the motel. One of the two men pointed at me. He looked like he was angry that I had gotten out of the motel and onto the street.

I made a turn at the next corner and drove down the street several blocks. I then turned again and quickly drove down that street a couple of blocks before I turned again.

After that last turn, I suddenly found myself in a small city park with no way out of the park except for the way I came in. I made a sharp U turn, and headed back out onto a city street.

At the first corner I came to I turned again. This time I found myself back on what looked like a main street into a business district. I found a gas station and pulled around behind it so my Explorer was out of sight of the main street. I raised the hood, then I walked around to the front of the gas station and went into the office. The station attendant looked up at me from behind his counter.

"Can I help you?"

"I'm just waiting for someone. Do you mind?"

"No, not at all."

"Thank you."

I stood near the door where I could watch the street, but where it would be very difficult to be seen by anyone driving by, or pulling into the station at the pumps.

It wasn't long before I saw the two men in a blue sedan cruise on by. It was clear that they were looking for me.

If they saw my Explorer, they apparently didn't think anything about it. With the hood up, they probably thought it was there being worked on, which was what I hoped they would think and continue to look for me.

I waited for awhile to make sure they were not just going around the block to come back to see if my vehicle was still there. It took almost five minutes before they came back and drove by the gas station again. They didn't stop in, although they did slow down and look at it. They must have decided that it was not the Explorer they were looking for, because they sped off.

I waited almost fifteen minutes to make sure they weren't going to drive by again. Once I was sure they were not going to return, I thanked the station attendant and left the gas station office. After putting the hood down, I drove it around to the gas pumps and filled the tanks. I paid for the gas and drove out of the gas station. I headed back in the opposite direction the men in the blue sedan had taken.

With the blue sedan no longer following me, it was time to make a call on Mrs. Smith. This time I would go to the back gate hoping that she would come out that way. The back gate also offered me a faster way to get out of the area if I needed to make a run for safety. I would call her while I was at the back gate.

I arrived at the Smith Estate about ten-thirty in the morning. I pulled off on the side of the street just down the drive from the back gate. I could see that it was Neil Upton in the guardhouse at the back gate.

I placed a call to Mrs. Smith using the phone number of the phone she had used to call me in Madison. The phone rang only twice before it was answered. As luck would have it, Barbara Smith answered the phone.

"Hello."

"Barbara, this is Nick McCord."

I thought I could hear a slight gasp. I was sure that my call had caught her by surprise.

"Ah – Yes, Mr. McCord. What can I do for you?"

"You can give me a few minutes of your time. It is important that you talk with me, alone. I do not want Josh to hear what I have to say to you."

"All right. I'll tell the guard at the gate to let you in."

"That won't do. Since I don't wish to be interrupted, I would like you to meet me on the street just outside the back gate, now."

"I don't understand."

"Let me just say that I don't think Josh is working for your best interest."

"I see."

There was a long pause before she said anything.

"Okay. I'll be there shortly."

"Thank you."

I kept a good watch of everything around me. I didn't want any surprises, like someone coming up behind me. I kept the engine running in case I had to make a hasty departure from the area.

It wasn't but a few minutes before I saw Barbara walking quickly down the drive toward me. She kept looking back toward the house. I wasn't sure if she was hoping she was being followed, or if she was trying to make sure she got out of the house and off the grounds without being seen. I didn't see anyone around or anyone following her. However, I did notice that Neil was keeping an eye on her as she walked toward me. I also noticed that she walked by Neil without saying anything.

When she got close to my vehicle, I motioned for her to get in on the passenger's side. I reached across the vehicle and pushed the door open for her.

"Get in. We'll talk here where I know we will have some privacy."

She got in the vehicle, shut the door, then turned and looked at me.

"What's going on?"

"You hired me to find out if the death of your husband was an accident or murder. Is that right?"

"Yes, I did. Did you find the answer to that question?"

"Yes. I believe it was murder, and I think I can prove it.

She didn't say anything for a few seconds.

"I had a feeling he was murdered," she said softly.

She looked like she was about to cry. I wasn't sure if it was real, or if she was faking it.

"My question to you is, did you also hire me to find out who caused the crash? In short, who murdered your husband?"

She looked at me as if I had asked a stupid question.

"Yes. Yes, I did. Do you know who murdered him?"

"I'm afraid not, but I'm working on it."

"You indicated Josh was not to be trusted. Do you think he murdered Brandon?"

"At this time, I don't know who murdered Brandon. I do know that someone close to you, and probably close to your husband, was involved in it, if not an actual participant."

"Do you have some idea who it is?"

"Yes, but I'm not ready to say. I don't have any proof. I prefer to have proof before I say anything."

"I understand," she said.

She sat looking out the windshield for a moment. I got the impression she was thinking, about what, I didn't know. She suddenly turned and looked at me again.

"What can I do to help?"

"You can't continue as if you never talked to me. I'm sure it will get around that you did talk to me. I will continue to work on it in an effort to find out who is involved, and what was the motive behind the murder of your husband."

"I'm sure my coming here to talk to you will get around rather fast," she said. "After all, Neil Upton saw me come here. He was hired by Josh and tends to report to Josh."

"Just tell them I was updating you on my investigation of whether or not Brandon was murdered. By the way, do you know that Russell Larson was murdered?"

I kind of sprung it on her on purpose. I wanted to see her reaction. From the expression on her face, I doubted that she knew about his death. Her body language also indicated that she didn't know he was dead. I decided that I would not inform her of any of the details, at least not yet.

"When? I just talked to him yesterday afternoon."

"What time did you talk to Russell?"

"Oh – it was about two-thirty yesterday afternoon. It might have been closer to two or two-fifteen. I'm not real sure. I talked to him on the phone for about fifteen minutes, certainly not more than that. I haven't seen or talked to him since."

"What did you talk about?"

"He talked about the Ferrari. We talked about Brandon and the car. Russell thought he would take one more look at the car to see if he might have missed something. He never called me back."

"Did he indicate what he thought might have been missed?"

"No. I think he wanted to be sure something important was not overlooked."

"The police are investigating Russell's death. They have not determined a time of death, yet. The last I heard was they are taking the car and trailer to the police forensic lab to examine it for evidence.

"You better get back to the house. We don't want anyone to get the idea we were discussing anything other than what I was hired to find out. If asked, that is what you tell them."

"Yes. I won't tell them anything different. I won't even say a word about Russell being dead. I hope you can find out why Brandon was murdered, and who did it.

"I'll tell anyone who asks that you still don't know if it was murder or an accident," she added.

"Okay. I'll keep in touch."

"Thank you, Mr. McCord."

Barbara got out of my vehicle, shut the door then started to walk back to the house. She walked much slower going back. I watched her until she was out of sight. As soon as she was gone, I slipped my vehicle into drive, then headed for the Calumet City Police station to talk to Joe Martin.

Upon my arrival at the Calumet City Police station, I went directly to the Desk Sergeant. It didn't take but a minute or so for the Desk Sergeant to call Joe, then direct me to Joe's office. I knocked on the door.

"Come in."

"How's it going?" I asked.

"It's going well. I didn't expect to see you here. How is it going with you?"

"I had a talk with Barbara Smith a little while ago. I get the feeling that she had nothing to do with the death of her husband. Now, don't hold me to that. She just might be a very good actress."

"Do you think talking to her was a good idea?"

"I don't know. She did say that she talked to Russell yesterday afternoon between two and two-thirty. Have you figured out when he was killed?"

"Not really, but the ME thinks it was between three and four in the afternoon."

"That would be about right. I arrived at the plant about four in the afternoon. The blood on the floor was fairly fresh at that time. I'm sure he was killed shortly before I found him. The time between when I arrived at the plant and you came to the plant kind of supports that idea."

"Yes, it does. But it doesn't eliminate her as a suspect."

I had to agree with him even if I didn't say so. It certainly was possible that she had killed him, or had him killed. Russell had been hit on the back of the head with a very heavy wrench, but not so heavy a wrench that a woman couldn't use it to hit a man on the head.

The wrench could have been a weapon of convenience. The large tool box that I had used when I first examined the car was sitting just outside the paint booth when I left. The wrench that was used to kill Russell could have been in that tool box.

It was possible that if the wrench was a weapon of convenience, and I had shown up about that time, the person who used it to kill Russell may not have had time to wipe it clean.

"Did your people find any prints on the wrench?"

"We found two, but have not identified them yet."

"Will you let me know who's fingerprints they are when you find out?"

"Yes. I had a talk with the chief. He is still willing to let me work with you. However, he did say that he hoped there wouldn't be any more bodies."

"I certainly hope there are no more bodies."

"When do you expect to get your reports on the bolts and the metal plate?"

"The last time I talked to the professor, it is going to be probably Monday or Tuesday."

"We have the Ferrari, and the trailer it was on, in our garage. The forensic team is working on it. Do you have anything else you consider evidence?"

"No, not at this time. I would like you to check to see if Barbara Smith made a call to Russell on the day she said. If she did, I'd like to know what time she made the call."

"I'll follow up on that and let you know what I find out."

"Between you and me, I have several people I think might be involved in the death of Brandon. I have Monica working on a couple of them."

"Who are they?" Joe asked.

"I'd rather not say. I don't want to make waves until I'm pretty sure of my information."

"Okay, but don't keep me in the dark much longer. I need some answers, and I need them soon. The chief is getting a little nervous about you having most of the evidence, and you don't seem to be sharing it with us. We need answers."

"I don't know if I have most of the evidence or not. The Ferrari may provide more evidence. I can assure you that you will get answers as soon as I get them."

I told Joe I would see him later and left the Calumet City Police station. It was time for me to find a motel to stay for tonight. I needed to contact Monica to see what she might have come up with since I last talked to her.

I decided that I would leave Calumet City and get a motel somewhere out of town. There was less chance of being spotted if I went out of town. I pointed my vehicle west and left town.

CHAPTER NINETEEN

I left Calumet City, drove to interstate 94, then took it south. I got off the interstate at the South Holland exit. It didn't take me long to find a fairly nice motel. Once at the motel, I parked off to the side then went inside to get a room. I was lucky and got a room that allowed me to keep an eye on my vehicle, not that I expected to have a problem there, but it didn't hurt to be cautious.

As soon as I had checked in, I went to my room and plugged in my computer. I then phoned Monica. She answered the phone rather quickly.

"This is Mrs. Wilma van Hunt. How my I help you?"

"Hi Wilma. This is Randolph van Hunt, our cousin from Florida."

"Oh, hi. I'm in the middle of something right now. Could I call you back in – say – forty-five minutes?"

"Sure. I look forward to it," I said then hung up.

"I had no idea what was going on, but I was sure there was someone else nearby. A quick look at my watch showed me that she was probably sitting at the table in the lodge having dinner.

Forty-five minutes gave me time to go to the little restaurant next door to the motel. Since it didn't seem very busy when I walked in the door, I figured I had time to get something to eat and still get back to my room before Monica called me back.

The waitress came to my table and gave me a menu. I picked today's special which was meatloaf with green beans and a choice of potatoes. Since I happen to like meatloaf, and the special is usually served quicker, I was sure I would have plenty of time to enjoy my dinner. It didn't take very long before the waitress returned with my dinner. It was actually very good.

After I finished my dinner, I returned to my room to wait for Monica to call me back. I didn't have to wait long. I picked up the phone after only two rings.

"Hello."

"Is everything okay on your end?" Monica asked.

"I think so. I've been thinking about Russell."

"What about Russell?"

"I was wondering why someone thought it necessary to kill him."

"Do you think Russell might have discovered something that could point a finger at who killed Brandon?"

"I don't know, it's possible. What I do know is Russell must have thought the Ferrari held more evidence. Apparently, someone thought he found something that would connect them to the crash of the car. There's also the possibility that someone felt he already knew too much and wanted to make sure he didn't tell anyone.

"Russell was hit from behind with a heavy wrench while he was looking at the Ferrari. It almost had to be someone he knew and didn't think he had anything to worry about, or he never would have turned his back to his killer." I said.

"That makes a lot of sense, but do you think you know who it might be?"

"No. I can think of several people who might have a reason to kill him, but nothing solid."

"Are you being careful?"

"Yes. I'm not in Calumet City right now. I left there. I figured it would be too easy to find me there. I'm in South Holland. It's about twenty to twenty-five miles from Calumet City."

"That was probably a good idea."

"I think we're getting close to someone, or at least we have made someone very nervous."

"You be careful."

"I will. Do you have anything new for me?" I asked.

"Yes, I think so. I've discovered that Stoker goes to the Cayman Islands every month. It seems that it happens on the same day of each month, each and every month for the past ten or eleven months at least. I have no idea what it means, but I found it suspicious."

"What day of the month?"

"Always on the second Tuesday of the month."

"Do you have any idea why the second Tuesday of the month?"

"No," Monica replied. "It might have something to do with some kind of payment, or to make a deposit in the company."

"Does he go alone, or does he go with someone?"

"As far as I can tell, he goes alone. I do know that he never takes his wife on those trips."

"That's interesting. I wonder if she has any idea what he is doing on those once a month trips?"

"I doubt it. I doubt she even knows where he is going," Monica said.

"You might be right. By the way, remember when we found the business in the Caymans?" I asked.

"Yes. What about it?"

"I don't think the second 'S' in the name of the company is for Smith? Everything I have found about Brandon's business, and the slow and careful takeover of it, points to Barbara not knowing a thing about it."

"Do you have any idea who the 'S' stands for?" Monica asked.

"No, not yet. I don't think she knows why, or who, killed Brandon. However, I'm not eliminating her as a suspect, just yet. When I talked to her in private, she assured me that she still wanted me to find out who killed her husband. She sounded very believable."

"I'll look into her a little more," Monica said. "I'll see if I can find anything that might help."

"Good idea. Have you been able to find anything more on Stoker? Something that might help us? If you can find out who some of his friends are and what they do, it might help."

"I'll work on that. I did find out that he is an officer on the board of one of the local country clubs. Two of the other officers are George Moorhouse and a judge by the name of Franklin P. Stevenson. He's on the bench in Chicago."

"Good going. See what you can find on him. I would like to know everything you can find on Stevenson."

"You think he might be the last 'S' we are looking for?"

"It's possible. Also see if he ever travels with Stoker to the Caymans, or travels there at the same time. You might also try to find out what airlines Stoker uses."

"Okay. I'll start looking tonight," Monica said. "What is your next move?"

"I'm planning to have a talk with Josh Ellis in the morning. I'd like to shake him up a bit."

"You be careful around him. He's smart and might be very dangerous."

"I have no doubt you are right. I'm hoping to get him to leak out something, hopefully without realizing it. At the very least, I hope to get him to make a mistake. I may put off talking to Josh until after I have a talk with Professor Houzerman."

"I agree. It might be better to talk to Professor Houzerman before you talk to Ellis," Monica suggested. "He might have some information for you that could help."

"I think you're right. I'll change my plans and go back to Madison to talk to Professor Houzerman. I need to know what he has found out about the parts we left with him. He may have found something that will make Ellis nervous," I said.

"Will you call me when you get done talking to the professor?"

"Yes. Do you have anything else for me?"

"No, nothing except that I love you and I want you to be careful."

"I will. I love you," I said.

"I love you, too," Monica said then she hung up.

I hung up the phone, then sat there for a minute looking at it. I really didn't want to hang up, but there was nothing more to say. I really was missing being with her at the Gill's Point Lodge.

It was time to get some rest, but I wanted to watch the news. I turned on the television to watch a little news. It seemed that it was the same thing every day. That was until they got to the local news. I was suddenly very much interested in the news when the reporter on the television screen started to speak into the mic in his hand. I could see the Smith Estate in the background.

"Early this evening, a rather large truck ran into the back guardhouse of the Brandon Smith Estate, killing the security guard inside the guardhouse. We have just been advised that the security guard was Neil Upton, a twenty-seven year old who worked as a guard to help pay for his schooling. Mr. Upton was an Army veteran who got out of the service just a little over a year ago. According to his employer, Mrs. Brandon Smith, Upton was saving up his money so he could continue his education.

"I was told by a reliable source that the brakes failed on the truck. The driver of the truck has been taken into custody for questioning, but the police have not arrested him or released the driver's name.

"This is the second tragedy to strike this home in recent weeks. Mrs. Smith lost her husband in a freak accident while racing his vintage Ferrari after his car had won 'Best of Show' at a car show in Chicago."

The newscast returned to the studio. There were no more comments on the "accidental death" of Neil.

It became apparent that the news didn't make mention of the death of Russell Larson. It occurred on property that belonged to Brandon Smith, though not on the estate. I decided that I didn't need to listen to any more of the news when the reporter signed off, and it went back to the station for other news.

Since I had not heard any news of Russell's death, I could only assume that either it was not considered newsworthy, or someone chose not to broadcast it. I kind of think it was the latter.

I wondered what it was that got Neil killed. What did he know? Was it something that could be harmful to someone, or what did whoever had him killed think he knew? Those were the questions I wanted answers to, but doubted I would get the answers anytime soon.

It was time for me to get some rest. I took a shower and then turned in for the night. It took me awhile to finally fall asleep.

I woke when the sun started to come in between a gap in the drapes. I had no more than gotten dressed and was ready to leave the motel when my phone began to ring. As far as I knew, no one other than Monica knew where I was. I reached over and picked up the receiver.

"Hello?"

"Is this Mr. Nick McCord?"

"Who are you?"

"Is this Mr. Nick McCord?"

It took a couple of seconds for it sink in. I quickly hung up the phone, grabbed my luggage and ran to the door. I carefully opened the door and peeked out. There was no one in the hall. I left the room and ran down the hall to a side exit that was on the opposite side of the building than my vehicle.

I hid my luggage in among some shrubbery, then carefully worked my way to the end of the building. When I looked around the corner, I could see a man in a dark suit standing close to my vehicle. He was looking toward the side entrance of the motel with his hand under his suit jacket. He must have been expecting me to come out that way.

I took a minute to look around and to figure out what I should do. In looking around, I saw that same blue sedan I had seen several times before. It was parked near my vehicle. It was backed into the parking space so it could get out quickly, most likely in case I got to my vehicle first.

If I could get to their car without being seen, I might be able to disable it. The problem was, I would need to take out the guy standing next to my vehicle.

While watching the guy, I quickly ran to the other side of the parking lot and ducked down behind a car. As soon as I was sure I had not been seen, I worked my way toward the blue sedan by staying behind parked cars.

It didn't take but a couple of minutes to get behind the blue sedan. I moved up alongside the sedan, then reached down and took the valve cover off the valve stem of one of the rear tires. I took a small stick from the bushes behind the car and jammed it down so it held the valve open allowing the air to escape from the rear tire. With my gun in my hand, I moved alongside the sedan until I was almost within reach of the man watching the door.

He must have heard the slight hissing from the air escaping out of the tire because he started to turn around. When he did, he found me with my gun pointed right at his face. He froze.

"One word, or sound from you, and you will have a big hole in your body. Turn around put your hands on the top of the car and spread 'um. I'm sure you know the drill."

He did as I requested. I quickly relieved him of his gun and the keys to the car. I tossed the keys off in the bushes, then quickly laid the butt of my gun across the back of his head causing him to fall to the ground. He was out cold.

I stepped over him, then ran to my vehicle and jumped in. As I was just pulling away, his partner came out of the motel. I quickly turned the corner around the end of the building.

Once around the corner, I made a quick stop. It was just long enough to pick up my luggage I had left behind a bush and toss it into my vehicle.

I glanced in my rearview mirror in time to see the man come around the corner of the building as I drove away. There was little doubt that the guy was mad as hell. It crossed my mind that I would see him again, and he would not be very friendly.

I was pretty sure that I would not be followed for a little while. At least one of them would have a splitting headache once he came around.

CHAPTER TWENTY

As soon as I got back to interstate 94, I headed south toward interstate 80, then west on interstate 80 to where I turned north on interstates 39 and 90 to Madison. I knew it was the long way around, but I wanted time to think without having to worry about being followed, at least for a while. I knew when I got close to Madison, I would have to keep my eyes open for the blue sedan or anyone else who might be following me.

My thoughts turned to what had happened at the motel. I had the feeling the two men who had been showing up all the time would expect me to return to my apartment in Madison. With that thought in mind, I drove directly to the University of Wisconsin's Engineering Department. I found a parking place near the end of the Engineering Department building in a parking lot that was away from the front door of the building.

Being careful in the hope of seeing the two men before they saw me, I worked my way between cars in the parking lot. I found a side door into the building where Professor Houzerman had his office and lab. I entered the building and walked down the hall to the professor's office.

I took a look around before entering the professor's office. I didn't see anyone who might be a threat to me. In fact, I didn't see but a few people who looked like students. Classes were probably over for the day. As I entered the office, Professor Houzerman's secretary looked up and smiled.

"Good afternoon, Mr. McCord."

"Good afternoon. Is Professor Houzerman available to talk to me?"

"I'm sure he is. He is in the lab. I'll get him for you."

"Thank you."

I watched the young woman as she stood up, turned and walked through a door that had sign on it. The sign read, "Laboratory".

While I waited for her return, I turned and looked out the window. My attention was quickly drawn to a green sedan that was just turning into a parking space in front of the building. It was the same make and model as the blue car I left behind with a flat tire at the motel in South Holland.

I noticed one of the two men getting out of the car was one of the men I saw at the motel in South Holland. He was the one I left standing in front of the motel as he watched me drive away. The one I had hit on the back of the head was probably licking his wounds somewhere back in Illinois.

The two men looked around then one of them pointed to the front door of the building. They turned and started walking toward the building.

Not wanting to have to confront them here, I turned and went through the door the professor's secretary had gone through. I found her talking to Professor Houzerman. They had a surprised look on their faces when I entered the room.

"Sorry to break in on you like this, but there are two men coming to your office that you do not wish to see. They are not friendly."

"What do you suggest?" Professor Houzerman asked.

"Is there a back way out of here?"

"Yes."

"Then let's use it."

Professor Houzerman and his secretary started for the backdoor. I noticed that the professor grabbed some papers off the desk next to the door as we left.

The backdoor led into a long narrow hallway. I followed along behind them as they hurried down the hall. When the professor made a sharp turn into a room, I followed. I stopped at the door and looked back down the hall to see if they might be following us. I didn't see anyone. I quickly closed the door.

"What's going on, Nick?" Professor Houzerman asked.

"I'm not sure, but if I have to guess, they are after the evidence I left with you to examine. That tells me they might be afraid that it could be used against whoever they are working for."

"Do you think we are in danger?"

"I hope not. Are the pieces of evidence sitting around in your lab?"

"No. They are locked up in my safe. I have the reports on them," he said as he held up the papers I had seen him grab on our way out of the lab.

"Good."

"Nick, you have a lot more experience in matters like this than I have. Do you think that if I was to tell them I have already turned the evidence over to the police they would leave and not bother me again?"

"They might, Professor, and they might not. I would prefer not to take the chance. These are not nice men, nor are they prone to taking someone's word for anything. Is there a phone in this room? I left mine in the car."

"This is a locker room for staff to store their coats and lunches. There aren't any phones in here," the Professor said.

"My phone is in my locker," his secretary said.

"May I use it?"

"Sure."

I watched as the professor's secretary went to a locker, opened it and got her phone out of her purse. She handed it to me. I quickly placed a call to Lieutenant Gerrie Baker. The call was transferred to her office. She answered the phone within a couple of minutes.

"Lieutenant Baker."

"Gerrie, this is Nick McCord. I need your help."

"What's up."

"I'm at the University of Wisconsin's Engineering Department building where Professor Houzerman has been examining some evidence. We are hiding in the building. There are two men in the building looking for us. They have been following me. They tried to catch me in South Holland, Illinois, this morning."

"I'll get a car over there as fast as I can. I'll also call the campus police and let them know what is going on."

"They are driving a green sedan," I said, then gave her the license plate number. "By the way, I am armed and will protect Professor Houzerman and his secretary."

"Good. I'm on my way," Lieutenant Baker said then the phone went dead.

I turned and looked at the professor and his secretary. I could see that they were scared, but I couldn't blame them. I reached out and handed the phone back to the professor's secretary.

"Thank you for the use of your phone. I don't think we have ever been properly introduced. My name is Nick McCord," I said.

I smiled and held out my hand in the hope it would help relieve some of her fears.

She looked at me as if I was a very strange person. After a moment, she reached out and took my hand.

"I'm Diana Summers," she said with a smile.

"It's nice to meet you, Miss Summers. The police will be here soon."

"It's Mrs. Summers."

"I guess you have gotten yourself into quite a mess," Professor Houzerman said.

"I think that is an understatement. I'm hoping you will help me get out of it. Is there anything in the items I asked you to examine that might help?"

Before the professor could answer my question, I could hear the sound of sirens.

It was only a short time later when we heard someone calling my name. It didn't sound like Lieutenant Baker. It sounded more like a man. It was either the men looking for us, or one of the policemen. I couldn't be sure which.

"I think we've been rescued," Diana said.

"I'm not so sure."

I waited and listened. There was a soft knock on the door. I decided not to answer it."

"This is the police. Is anyone in there?" the voice asked.

"Hello, this is Gerrie. Are you in there?"

I smiled at the sound of her voice.

"Yes, Lieutenant Baker," I said as I opened the door.

She entered the room and looked at the three of us.

"Are you all right?"

"We are now," I said as I slipped my gun under my sport coat.

"You want to tell me what's going on?"

"Yes. This is Professor Houzerman and his secretary, Mrs. Diana Summers."

"Nice to meet you," Gerrie said.

"It is certainly nice to meet you," Professor Houzerman said with a grin.

"Nick, you want to tell me what is going on?"

"Professor Houzerman was just getting ready to tell me the results of his examination of the evidence I found when I examined the vintage Ferrari that Brandon Smith was driving when he was murdered."

"Then you are sure it was murder?" she asked.

"Yes. Professor Houzerman was just about to tell me what he found in his examination of the evidence I had given him. Why don't we let him tell both of us as the same time? Professor."

"Thank you, Nick. There is no question that the bolts used on the Ferrari to secure the front wheel assembly to the frame were not the right kind of bolts. They were damaged, but I was able to connect them to the ends of the bolts you gave me later. It was clear under a microscope that the bolts had been further weakened before they were attached to the car."

"So, you can prove the suspension had been tampered with, is that right?" Lieutenant Baker asked.

"Definitely. The problem is finding out who tampered with them," Professor Houzerman quickly reminded me.

"What about the seatbelt harness? Was it tampered with?" I asked.

"Yes. The latch that secures the shoulder straps across the chest and the latch across the lap of the driver are held by metal clamps designed to be able to be released quickly. They are made that way to make it easier to get someone out of the car quickly in case of an accident, but not open unless opened by hand.

"In this case, the edges of the clamp where the two parts fit together had been shaved, or rounded off, weakening the ability to remain connected under stress."

"The head mechanic told me that he had helped Brandon get buckled in. He told me that they were snug and held tight when he pulled on them to make sure they were properly hooked," I said.

"Normally, pulling on them would not have caused them to come apart. They could only be opened by using both hands to release the latch. It would have to be done by someone pulling the latch apart. However, in this case the edges of the clamps had been shaved so there was very little metal holding them together," Professor Houzerman explained.

"So, when the car hit the guardrail, Brandon's body was slammed against the harness popping open the harness and throwing him out of the car. Is that right?" I asked.

"That's right," Professor Houzerman confirmed.

"I guess that proves it was murder," Lieutenant Baker said. "But what was the motive?"

"I have a couple of thoughts on that, but have not been able to prove either one, yet," I said. "I have Monica working on that in a place where she is safe."

"Will you let me know what you come up with?" Gerrie asked.

"I will as soon as we get it figured out."

"Okay."

"What about the two men who I called about. Do you have them?"

"Yes. We have them, but they are not talking. I will probably have to release them when their attorney finds out we have them. What we are holding them on makes it hard to keep them from being released on bail. By the way, one of them is the same guy we arrested for entering your home," Gerrie added.

"I was pretty sure that I had seen that one before. With the sunglasses he was wearing, I couldn't be sure," I said.

After Lieutenant Baker's officers got all our statements, she left with the other officers. I decided to go to a motel even though I was only a short distance from my apartment. I said goodbye to Professor Houzerman and Mrs. Summers then left.

I drove to a small motel on the outskirts of Madison and registered for the night. It was fairly late and I had not had anything to eat. There was a little café just across the street. It didn't look like much, but it was close. I walked across the street to the café.

I had a peaceful meal, if not the best meal I have ever had. When I finished, I returned to the motel and placed a call to Monica. She answered the phone rather quickly.

"Hi, Honey," she said.

"Hi, how is it going?"

"I think I've found something interesting."

"What's that, Honey?"

"I think I might have found out what the single 'S' stands for. I think it stands for Stevenson, as in Franklin P. Stevenson, the judge."

"What leads you to believe that?"

"Several things. First of all, he appears to be a close friend of Stoker. Secondly, they play golf regularly and are both on the country club's board. Third, he has flown several times to the Caymans on the same plane as Stoker. When they fly on the same plane, they purchase separate tickets and don't sit together.

Stevenson doesn't fly down there regularly; but he has been there five times in the past year, and each time it was at the same time as Stoker."

"That's very interesting."

"I've got more. It looks like Stevenson is also into vintage cars. He owns a 1932 Duesenberg Roadster that he inherited from his father who was also a judge. He has been known to show it from time to time, but apparently only in a few shows close to Chicago."

"I would say that Stoker and Stevenson just might be very good friends. Is there any indication that Stoker has been in front of Stevenson in court?"

"I haven't found anything like that, yet. I'll work on it and see what I can find."

"You might want to take a close look at Moorhouse. He's involved in all this somehow. I just don't know how. I don't think he's a big player, but he knows a lot about what is going on. See if you can find something I can hold over him that might make him a little more willing to talk to me. He doesn't strike me as the type to want to go to jail for something someone else did."

"Okay. How are things going for you?" Monica asked.

"We have proof that it was murder. Now all we have to do is figure out who killed Brandon and why."

"That should be a 'piece of cake'." Monica said with a chuckle in her voice. "What's your next move?"

"I'm going back to Calumet City tomorrow to visit the forensic lab at the police building in Calumet City. I want to see if they have found anything that might help me. I got a feeling there is something more the car can tell us."

"You think that is why Russell was killed?" Monica asked.

"It seems logical. What other reason would he have to go back and see the car again. And what other reason would someone have for killing him?"

"I don't know of any. I see your point."

"Once I get done at the forensic lab, I'm going to Chicago to pay a visit to Moorhouse."

"You be careful. Moorhouse has a lot to lose, that could make him dangerous."

"I will. I think I'll call it a day and get some rest. How are things going at the lodge?"

"Good. I miss having you here. I like to take walks along the shore after dinner. The people here are nice and friendly. It's nothing like when we were here before," Monica said.

"I wish I could be there, too. I'll call you tomorrow."

"Okay. Love you."

"I love you, too. Goodnight, Honey."

"Goodnight," she said then hung up the phone.

I sat there looking at the phone for a moment or two, wishing I was there to take walks along the beach with her. But that would have to wait.

It was getting late and I needed to get some rest. I took a shower then went directly to bed. It didn't take me long to fall asleep.

CHAPTER TWENTY-ONE

The sun had come up and was shining into my room. It looked like it might be a nice day. I swung my legs over the side of the bed and got up. After shaving and getting dressed, I packed my luggage. I was about to leave my room when the phone began to ring. I answered the phone, all the time wondering who was calling me here. I hadn't told anyone where I was staying, not even Monica.

"Hello?"

"Mr. McCord, this is Alfred Winters at the front desk. I'm the manager of this motel. Are you planning on checking out this morning?"

"Why do you ask?"

It seemed like a strange question to me.

"There was a man here asking about you."

"Oh. Did he tell you his name?"

"No, sir."

"Did he tell you what he wanted?"

"No, sir. He just asked if you were registered here. He concerned me a bit, though."

"Why were you concerned?"

"When he came in, I noticed that he had a gun under his sport coat. He had that look, you know, like he was afraid that someone might see him who he didn't want to see him. I knew he was not a police officer. They always look confident and like they know what they're doing. They also identify themselves, he didn't.

"I told him that we didn't have any McCord registered here at the moment. He did say that he saw your car parked out back."

"When he told you he saw my car, what did you tell him?"

"I told him that you had checked out early this morning and left with someone in a red Ford sedan. I also told him that I thought you would probably be back to pick up your car later, but I had no idea when you would be back to pick it up."

"Is he still around?"

"Yes, sir. He's sitting in a car just behind your car."

"How do you know that?"

"We have security cameras in the halls and around the outside of the building that covers the parking lot. I'm looking at him right now. I had seen him looking at your car shortly before he came in. That's what drew my attention to him when he walked in the door."

"That was good thinking, Mr. Winters. Thanks."

"What do you plan to do about it?"

"I plan to let him wait there. You said he is out back where my Explorer is parked?"

"Yes, sir."

"Okay. This is what I would like you to do. Keep me registered as McCord to this room. If he should come back in and ask, tell him I changed my mind and called you to keep the room available. Okay?"

"Yes, sir.

"Good. Now, would you be so kind as to register me as Randolph van Hunt in another room, then have one of your people bring me the key card to that room. I'd like the room to be where I can see my Explorer, if you can arrange it. I'll move to that room. I probably won't be staying here tonight, but keep both rooms available for me in case I need one of them. I will pay for both rooms for two nights. I will also leave my Explorer here. Do you understand?"

"Yes, sir. It is clear what you want me to do. I'll do it right away."

"Thank you, Mr. Winters."

"Please call me, Alfred."

"Okay, Alfred. Is there some way you can get me out of here without him seeing me?"

"Yes, sir. I'll have our van brought around to the front of the motel. You can get in it and I'll take you wherever you want to go."

"Good. Call me when you are ready."

"Excuse me for asking, sir, but does this man have something to do with one of your investigations?"

"What makes you ask that?"

"I happen to know you are a private investigator here in Madison. I'm told you are good at what you do."

"I see. Yes, and I don't want him following me."

"I understand," Alfred said.

"I would appreciate it if no one else knows about me staying here."

"I will keep it to myself, Mr. McCord. I'll take you where you want to go."

"Thanks," I said then hung up.

Without parting the curtains, I looked out through the crack between them. I could see a car with a man sitting in it parked a couple rows behind my Explorer. He was sitting in a gray car drinking from a cup. He looked like he had made himself comfortable as if he was expecting to be there for awhile. If it was up to me, he would be there for a very, very long time.

It wasn't but a few minutes before I heard a knock on the door. I walked over to the door and looked out through the peep hole. Alfred was standing in front of the door looking directly at the door and holding up a motel key card.

I opened the door and let him in. I checked the hall in both directions before shutting the door.

"This is your new room key card. The room is ready for you."

"Thank you, Alfred."

"I'll help you move your luggage, if you like."

"Thank you."

He picked up my luggage and started for the door. He stopped at the door and looked at me, waiting to see if I was ready to leave.

I looked around the room to make sure I didn't leave anything behind. Opening the door, I looked up and down the hall. There was no one in the hall. I motioned for him to follow me. We moved quickly down the hall to the new room. I unlocked the door and entered the room with Alfred right behind me.

"You can set that on the luggage rack," I said.

I went to the window and peeked out. The guy in the car was still there.

"Thanks for your help," I said.

"Will you be leaving soon?"

"I'd like to leave in a few minutes."

"I already have the van parked in front of the motel at the front door. I'm sure you can get in it without the man in the car being able to see you. I'll drive you personally.

"I usually take the van about this time in the morning to go to the bank. I'll carry my bank bag so it looks like I'm going to the bank," Alfred explained.

"Are you ready to go?"

"Yes, sir."

"Then I'll go with you."

I followed Alfred out of the room and made sure that the door locked behind us. Once we got to the front lobby, I could see the van parked right in front of the front doors. I followed him out and slipped into the van using the door for passengers while he walked around and got in the driver's seat. I laid down on the seat so no one could see I was in the van. It was only a matter of a couple of minutes and we were out on the street.

"I don't see anyone following us. Where would you like to go?" Alfred asked.

"I would like to go to my apartment," I said, then gave him the address. Since we were away from the motel, I sat up.

"Do you think that's a good idea? There might be someone watching it."

"Actually, we are going to the garage where I have a sports car. I won't actually be going to the apartment."

"Oh."

"When you drive into the parking lot, keep an eye out for a green or blue sedan. If you see it, drive on out as if you were in the wrong place."

"Okay."

I got the impression that Alfred was enjoying being what he probably considered a small part of playing "cat and mouse" with a suspect in what, he didn't know. I was glad I could make his day. I was sure he wouldn't see his job as the manager of a motel as interesting after today.

When we got to the apartment complex, I directed him to the location of the garage where we kept Monica's little sports car.

"Take a slow lap around the parking lot. Make it look like you're looking for an address."

"We're looking for the blue sedan, right?"

"Right, or a green one."

After we made a complete circle of the parking lot without seeing a green or blue sedan, I pointed to the garage. He pulled up in front of it so the van was between the garage door and the parking lot. He parked very close to the garage which would make it difficult for anyone to see what we were doing.

"Thanks, Alfred. You're a good man."

"You're welcome. Someday, maybe, you could tell me what this is all about?" he asked, hopefully.

"I'd be happy to tell you all about it when it is done. I'll see you later, and thanks for your help."

"You're welcome."

I got out of the van and opened the garage door. As soon as I had Monica's car started, Alfred drove the van out of the way so I could back out of the garage.

When I had the car out of the garage, Alfred closed the garage door. I waved a thank you, then drove out of the parking lot. A look in my rearview mirror showed me that Alfred was following me out to the street.

As soon as I was out on the street, I headed for Calumet City where the Ferrari had been taken, and where it would be inspected by a team of forensic specialist. I wanted to find out what they might have discovered that I missed. I didn't see anyone following me.

It was shortly before noon when I arrived in Calumet City. I went directly to the police garage where the Ferrari had been taken. I parked out in front and looked around before I went inside. I was greeted by Sergeant Miller, the team leader, in his office. We talked briefly then went to where the Ferrari had been inspected. It was no longer on the trailer, but had been taken off and was now on the floor.

"Detective Joe Martin told me you might be by, and that I was to answer any of your questions."

"I appreciate that. Have you completed your inspection of the car?"

"Yes, sir. We finished last night."

"What did you find?"

"Other than the fact that the car had been badly damaged by the crash into the guardrail, we found a bullet hole in the windshield."

"A bullet hole, in the windshield?"

"Yes sir."

"Was the bullet hole in the windshield where it might have hit the driver?"

"I don't think so. The windshield was made of Plexiglas, a fairly hard plastic, so it didn't shatter like a glass windshield would, that's the only reason we found it.

"Just to be sure, I called the ME to see if the driver had any injuries from a gunshot. He told us that the driver had not been shot. He did say that the driver having been thrown from the car and striking his head against the guardrail was the principal cause of death. He did say that the driver had a lot of bruises and a number of broken bones, but they were consistent with what would be expected in that type of accident."

"I found a fairly new gouge in the racetrack that looked like it had been made by a bullet. Could the same bullet, after passing through the windshield, have made the gouge in the pavement?" I asked.

"If it didn't hit anything else, it is possible, but not likely. We didn't find any bullet holes anywhere else on the car."

"Could the gouge in the pavement been caused by a bullet after it went through - say - a car tire while the car was moving?'

"Very unlikely. The gouge in the pavement might have been made by the rim of a wheel after a tire blew. We found two tires that were flat."

"Oh. Did you find anything else?"

"I understand that you examined the car in the plant where we picked it up. Is that correct?"

"Yes. I didn't see the bullet hole in the windshield, though."

"That might have been because it was low on the windshield and not easy to see until we pulled it up where the complete windshield could be seen."

"Oh."

"So, you saw the front wheel assembly had almost completely been broken off the frame?" Sergeant Miller asked.

"Yes. I also found three partial bolts that I had taken to a lab for examination. It was found that the bolts were the wrong ones for what they were used for, and that the bolts had been tampered with as well. There was also a small metal plate that was found at the site of the crash, but we have not been able to find out what it belonged to," I said.

"Was it about six inches long and about four inches wide and painted Ferrari red?"

"Yes."

"My guess it is from the bottom of this Ferrari. It covered a neatly cut out section in the bottom of the car. It was where the brake lines to the rear brakes joined with the main brake line. We found brake fluid around the opening. We checked with the Ferrari dealership in Chicago. One of the mechanics said there should not have been any kind of opening to the brake lines in the bottom of the car in that area. We examined the brake lines and the connections closely and found a small hole just above the joint coupling."

"What do you make of that?" I asked, already having a good idea of what it meant.

"I think that someone carefully cut out the piece of metal, tampered with the connection of the brake lines by drilling a small hole near the coupling. Once that was done, the metal plate was replaced by soldering it in place then painting over it so the cut out could not be seen. My guess would be that the metal plate apparently broke loose and fell off during the crash."

"That certainly sounds feasible. Even if Brandon wanted to stop the car quickly, he would not have been able to do it. Is that right?" I asked.

"That would be right," Sergeant Miller agreed. However, the leak was so small it would not affect normal braking right away. The brakes would have worked pretty much normally for a good part of the race. Someone knew what they were doing."

"I think you are right. Based on what you know about the car, what would you say was likely what happened?"

"Well," he said thoughtfully. "I think that the Ferrari was coming around the corner when a bullet passed throw the windshield, surprising the driver. That caused him to make a quick jerk of the steering wheel. That move put too much stress on the wheel mountings causing the wheel mountings to separate from the frame. That in turn caused the car to crash into the guardrail, throwing the driver out of the car. All that happened in a matter of just a couple of seconds."

"I would say this is definitely a case of murder."

"I would certainly agree with you," Sergeant Miller said. "I will have a written report for you, and for Detective Martin, later today. It will be evidence if and when you figure out who tampered with the car."

"Tell me this. Would the wheel mountings have broken if the right bolts had been used to join the wheel mountings to the frame?"

"I would have to say, probably not. The right bolts were made to withstand even the hardest of turns on that car."

As soon as I was finished talking to Sergeant Miller about the car and what he found, I thanked him and left.

I wanted to have a talk with Mr. George Moorhouse, so I headed for Chicago. It was my plan to put the fear of going to jail in him.

As I drove along in Monica's little sports car, I began to put what I had learned into perspective. I had a pretty good idea why Brandon had been murdered, but wasn't a hundred percent sure. It was most likely one of two reasons.

One reason was Stoker didn't like losing to Brandon at the car shows. With his temperament, I could see him going to such extremes to eliminate Brandon from ever showing his car again. I didn't know which was the objective, wrecking the car, or killing Brandon. Maybe he didn't care as long as he didn't have to deal with Brandon again. Stoker certainly had people close to him who would be willing to do whatever it took to put Brandon out of the car shows.

The second reason, and the one I suspected of being the main reason, was Brandon suspected that his business was being sold out from under him piece by piece. He had probably found out about the time of the show, but didn't know who was involved or how to prove it. He might even have been trying to find answers without anyone knowing, but someone figured it out and killed him to keep him from doing anything about it.

I started with several suspects, but two of them were now dead. It looked like one or more of my remaining suspects were involved in the murder, possibly several of them. William F. Stoker, Josh Ellis, Judge Franklin P. Stevenson and George Moorhouse were left, but I couldn't convince myself to eliminate Barbara Smith, not just yet. I sort of believed her, but not completely.

Barbara had a lot to gain from Brandon's death, plus I didn't know what her relationship to Josh Ellis might be. He was her personal assistant, but was he more than that? I wanted to know what kind of relationship they really had, and who he actually worked for. My guess was he worked for Stoker, but I couldn't prove it. I also wanted to know if there might be someone else involved that I didn't know about.

There were also the men who were working to stop me from finding the truth about Brandon's murder. The only thing was, I didn't know who they were or who they worked for. That was something I needed to find out. So far, everything I had been able to find out pointed at them as working for Stoker, but I was not able to prove it.

CHAPTER TWENTY-TWO

I arrived at the building where George Moorhouse had his law office. I parked in the building's underground parking garage in a visitor parking space near the exit, then walked to the front of the building.

Once inside the lobby, I looked for a directory and found it near the elevators. It didn't take more than a minute or so to find where Moorhouse and Associates Law Offices were located. They were on the ninth floor. From the look of the directory, Moorhouse's offices took most, if not all, of the ninth floor.

There was a bank of elevators off to the side of the directory. I went to the elevators, push the "up" button, then waited for the elevator to arrive. As soon as the doors opened, I stepped inside the elevator. As I turned around and reached for the button that would take the elevator to the ninth floor, I noticed a security officer watching me. The elevator was empty so I pressed the button for the ninth floor. The security officer watched me until the doors slowly closed. I thought to myself that he seemed a little too interested in me.

The lobby had only three people in it that I noticed. Two of them were security people, the other one looked like a janitor. I didn't see anyone that looked like a business person. It seemed strange that there didn't seem to be anyone around, especially for a weekday.

Once the elevator started to move, it took me to the ninth floor without any stops along the way. When the elevator stopped and the door opened, the first thing I saw was a reception counter with the name of the law firm on the front. It was directly in front of the elevator, but a good twenty feet from the elevator.

Sitting behind the counter was a well-dressed young woman. She looked up and smiled as I walked toward the counter.

"My I help you, sir?"

"Yes. I would like to speak to Mr. George Moorhouse, please."

"Do you have an appointment?"

"No, but I'm sure he will want to talk to me."

"I'm sorry, but he is not available to anyone without an appointment."

I was not surprised by her comment. I looked at her for a moment, then at the counter. There was a pad of paper on the counter with a pen lying beside it. I picked up the pen, took a sheet of paper off a pad and wrote a short note. I neatly folded the note and handed it to her.

"Please give Mr. Moorhouse this note. I'm sure he will want to talk to me."

She looked at the note, but didn't open it, then looked at me for a moment. At that point I wasn't sure she would give him the note. It wasn't until she stood up that my hope of seeing Mr. Moorhouse improved.

I watched as the young woman turned, then walked around behind a wall. I was sure it blocked the view of a hall that led to the offices of the lawyers. It wasn't but a couple of minutes before she returned. From the look on her face, I still wasn't sure if Moorhouse would talk to me.

"Mr. Moorhouse will see you. Right this way."

"Thank you."

I smiled to myself as I followed the young woman around behind the wall and down the hall to the office at the very end of the hall. She opened the door to Moorhouse's office, stepped back to allow me to enter the office. As soon as I was inside the office, she closed the door.

Sitting behind a rather large, very nice, probably a solid maple desk, was George Moorhouse. He rose and walked around to the front of the desk while I walked across the large room toward him.

"I see you have a way with words, Mr. McCord," Moorhouse said.

"I wanted to get your attention."

"Well, it worked. What's this about a murder? Didn't the Chicago police rule it an accident?" he said, then turned and walked around behind his desk.

He pointed to a chair in front of his desk. I sat down before I answered his question."

"Yes, they did. Let me put it this way. A thorough forensic examination of the 1954 Ferrari owned by Brandon Smith was done by the Calumet City Police Department. I was assured that there was absolutely no doubt that Brandon had been murdered. The forensic examination of the car showed that there is no doubt that the car had been tampered with causing it to crash, killing Brandon. The examination of the items I found when I looked at the car also showed that the suspension system had been tampered with, as well as the seatbelt harness."

I made it a point not to tell him about the bullet hole in the windshield.

The look on his face was blank, no sign of surprise, no sign of anything. I was sure he didn't expect the car to be looked at so closely. His expression was nothing less than what I expected from an attorney who was always dealing with criminals. I'm sure he practiced very hard at not showing his real feelings, or giving any hint of what he was thinking.

"Is this supposed to mean something to me?"

"At this point, I'm not sure what it means, but it won't be long before I have a pretty good idea who killed Brandon and why. I have a number of suspects. It seems that two of them have been eliminated already."

He looked at me for a moment before he spoke.

"What do you mean by 'eliminated'?"

It was obvious that the use of the word 'eliminated' got a slight reaction from him. He just might be getting a little nervous.

"I think 'killed', or maybe 'murdered', might be a better way of putting it."

"Who was killed?"

"You don't know?"

"No, I don't know. How would I know?"

He was showing signs of being shaken. I wondered if he might be afraid that he might be the next one 'eliminated'.

"In that case, I'll tell you. Russell Larson, Brandon's mechanic. He was found in the paint booth in the old plant with his head smashed in. He had been hit several times with a very large and heavy wrench. The police have the wrench for examination. They told me that it had a couple of fingerprints on it, but didn't know whose they were, yet."

I took a minute to just watch him, while I let it soak in. For all his practice at keeping his face from showing what he was really feeling, he wasn't doing so well on this one.

"Neil Upton, a security guard at the gate to the Smith estate had the misfortune to be run over by a rather large truck. The truck ran over him while he was in the back guardhouse at the Smith estate. He was crushed to death by the truck and the collapse of the guardhouse."

Mr. Moorhouse was having a difficult time keeping his cool now. His body language showed me that he might be a bit more than a little scared.

"I knew Upton," he said with a note of sadness in his voice.

If he was scared from what I had told him, I wondered how he would feel with my next comments. I continued.

"Oh, by the way, a guy by the name of Ricker, Billy Ricker, was also murdered. He wasn't even a suspect."

"I don't know anyone named Billy Ricker. What's his connection to this?"

"Billy Ricker was one of the members of the clean up crew at the racetrack. He was murdered simply because he found a couple of pieces of evidence that proved to be very valuable to my investigation. The poor man was beaten severely. His face looked like someone had used it for a punching bag, and the fingers of both his hands were broken. It was probably done to get him to tell where he had the pieces of evidence hidden. When he didn't talk, he was taken to the basement of his home where he was shot in the head. There's a lot of evidence from that scene that might be able to point to who did it. It shouldn't be too long before the police will find the men who did it.

"By the way, the forensic team found the evidence he had hidden. All of it has not been processed, yet. It sure will be interesting to find out what the evidence tells us. Those forensic people can find a needle in a haystack."

"I don't know any Ricker," Moorhouse repeated.

It was clear that he was scared. I could see little beads of sweat on his upper lip. I was sure that Moorhouse did not play a part in the murders, nor did he know about all of them. However, his voice showed he was becoming concerned. I didn't know if it was because he thought I might be getting close to figuring out who ordered the killings, or if he thought that he might be the next one to be found dead somewhere because he knew too much.

"You wouldn't happen to know who is responsible for any of these deaths?"

"Ah – NO, of course not. How would I know?"

"I just thought I would ask. You deal with a lot of lowlifes in your line of work. I thought you might have some idea who might be responsible. I'm sure I don't have to tell you that if you know something about any of these deaths and don't tell the police, you could be in a lot of trouble. Maybe, even lose your license to practice law, or go to jail."

"I don't' know anything about them. I think it is time for you to leave," he said as he stood up.

I knew I shook him up. His hands were shaking just bit, and he looked very uncomfortable. I was hoping he would make a mistake.

"Good day, Mr. Moorhouse."

I stood and looked at him for a couple of seconds, then turned and walked to the door. As I reached for the door, I stopped and turned toward him.

"You might want to be very careful. You never know when an accident might happen," I said with a grin.

I opened the door and left his office. I was sure he would be making a call to whoever was involved in the murders. I waited for just a second outside his door. Sure enough. I had no more than closed the door and I could hear him placing a call. I had no idea who he called, but it was time for me to get out of that building, and fast.

When the elevator arrived, I stepped in and pressed the button for the underground parking garage. When it got to the main floor, it stopped. The doors opened and a man in a dark suit stepped in. I got a chance to look him over before the elevator started to move.

Just as the elevator was about to stop in the underground parking garage, I slammed the man up against the wall of the elevator, pressing his face against the wall. I quickly relieved him of the gun he had under his coat, then threw the switch that prevented the doors from opening. He tried to object, but it didn't do any good.

"What do you think you're doing?" he said, his face still pressed hard against the wall of the elevator.

"Who the hell are you and who do you work for?"

"That's none of your business."

"Wrong answer."

Holding his gun firmly against his spine, I reached around him and took his wallet out of his coat pocket. Keeping the gun on his spine, I flipped open his wallet. His driver's license showed his name as Joseph Archer and he lived in Chicago.

"Mr. Archer, you are an employee of Moorhouse law firm it says here in your wallet."

"So what?"

"That tells me that George must have called you to meet me in the parking garage. Now why would he do that since I just talked to him?"

"Maybe you forgot something in his office."

"I guess I'll just have to leave you here."

Still keeping him pressed against the side of the elevator, and holding his gun on him, I reached around and unbuckled his belt. I pulled his belt from his pants then carefully moved him over to the handrail at the back of the elevator. I looped the belt around the handrail. With his hands in front of him, I pressed him against the handrail, then buckled his belt behind his back after pulling it up as tight as I could.

As soon as he was as secure as I could make him, I opened the elevator door. I backed out, then reached inside and pressed the button for the top floor of the building. I knew that it wouldn't take him long to get loose and get back to the underground garage, but by the time he did, I hoped to be gone.

As soon as the doors closed, I ran to my car, got in and drove out onto the street. I drove to the nearest police station and walked in the door with Archer's gun in my hand. I was holding it up by the barrel so no one would mistake me for someone who wanted to shoot up the place.

The Desk Sergeant saw me coming toward him. I noticed that he changed positions which was a good indication that he was ready if I changed my mind and decided to shoot up the place.

"There is nothing to worry about, Sergeant. I'm here to turn in a gun," I said as I raised my hand higher.

"My name is Nick McCord. I'm a private investigator from Madison, Wisconsin. I'm also licensed in Illinois.

I slowly stepped up to the desk and laid the gun on the counter where he could reach it, then stepped back a couple of steps, still keeping my hands in sight. The Desk Sergeant quickly took the gun. He quickly racked the gun open, removing a cartridge from the chamber, then removed the magazine.

"Is it okay if I reach inside my coat for my ID and permit to carry?"

"Okay, but do it slowly."

"Yes, sir."

Opening my coat so he could see what I was doing, I reached in my pocket for my ID and permit to carry. I handed them to the desk sergeant. He had just taken them when an officer walked into the room.

"Nick McCord, how the hell are you?"

I turned and looked at who had spoken to me. At the same time the Desk Sergeant looked up at me.

"Norm Walker. I wondered what happened to you when you left the force."

"I'm a detective here now. I heard you left Milwaukee and became a PI."

"Yeah."

Norm looked at the sergeant. The sergeant had a confused look on his face.

"What's going on here?" Norm asked.

"I take it you know this guy?" the Desk Sergeant asked.

"I sure do. We were street cops in Milwaukee. I left Milwaukee about the time he became a detective. I haven't seen him for several years."

"That seems like a lifetime ago," I said.

"It does. What's going on here?"

"It might be something that will concern you before long. Can we go someplace quiet where we can talk?"

"Sure."

"You might want this," the Desk Sergeant said.

Norm looked at the sergeant, then took the gun from him. I followed Norm to his office. He sat down behind his desk while I took a seat in front of it.

"You want to tell me what's going on?"

"Before we get into that, you might want to run tests on that gun. It might be involved in a murder in Calumet City."

"Okay. Now what's going on?"

I took my time telling him about the case I had been working on. Since I knew him to be a good cop, I didn't hold anything back. I led him through my investigation in chronological order, so he could get an idea of how I got involved and where my investigation had taken me so far. I even named names in the hope he could help me get information on them.

"Wow. When you take on an investigation, you take on a doozy. You're looking into some very influential people," Norm said.

"Yeah, so I've found out. I have just followed my leads."

"It looks to me like you have the makings of a good case against Stoker. We've been trying to pin something on him for years, but never seem to get anything that will stick."

"Right now, everything at this time is circumstantial. I'm lacking any solid proof."

"Maybe if we work together, we can put together a case against him that will stick," Norm suggested.

"I sure wouldn't mind the help. One of the problems I have is connecting the dots. I know of two men who are deeply involved in what has been happening. It would be great if I could get at least one of them to talk."

"Who are they?" Norm asked.

"Mr. George Moorhouse is one. I had a talk with him in his office. I think Moorhouse is the weakest link in the organization. My talk with him earlier shook him up.

"I must have hit a nerve. I scared him enough that he had one of his muscles try to get me on my way out. The gun you have, I took off him. His name is Joseph Archer."

"Who is the other one?"

"What can you tell me about Judge Franklin P. Stevenson?"

"He has been on the bench for a lot of years. He's probably getting up there where he wants to retire. He has a reputation as a hard, but fair judge."

"Well, I've been able to find out that Stevenson has close ties to Stoker. He has flown to the Cayman Islands five times in the past year at the same time, even on the same airplane as Stoker. I'm not sure it has anything to do with Stoker, although it is interesting that the only times he has gone to the Caymans have been at the same time Stoker goes," I said.

"Stevenson is also on the board of an antique auto club in Chicago and shows his antique car together at times with Stoker. He is also on the board of a local golf course with Stoker. They play golf together frequently. They obviously know each other and are most likely very good friends."

"That's more than I know about him. All I know about him is he has close ties to Stoker, but I couldn't find anything wrong about that. I'm sure they know a lot about each other," Norm said.

"I think it would be a good idea if I look into his financial records. Who knows, it might show something that will help," I said.

"If I do it here, someone might see it and get the idea I'm looking into him for some reason," Norm said. "There seems to be very little privacy here."

"You think there is someone here who is a mole?"

"I can't prove it, but we never seem to be able to get information on Stoker or any of his associates. Every time it looks like we might have something, it mysteriously disappears."

"I just might be able to get around that. I have just the person to get his financial records and do a background check on him for us."

"Anybody I know?"

"No, and that is what makes it perfect. No one knows her, except me. I'll talk to her tonight."

"It's a woman?"

"Yes."

"I take it you're not going to tell me anything about her," Norm said.

"That would be correct. Maybe sometime later. Right now, I've got to find a place to hold up tonight. I'll keep in touch."

"Okay."

I left the police station and got in my car. I made it a point to leave the city. I kept a close eye out for anyone who might be following me. I didn't see anyone, but to be on the safe side, I made a lot of stops and wound around a lot.

CHAPTER TWENTY-THREE

I drove out to one of the suburbs where I found a nice motel that looked like it might be privately owned. After parking my car, I went in to register. I filled out the registration card as Randolph van Hunt. Since I didn't have a credit card in that name, I asked to talk to the manager. The manager came out and I pulled him off to one side where no one could see us talking or hear us.

"I'm sorry to take your time, but I should explain what is going on here."

"It isn't anything illegal, is it?" he asked with a concerned look on his face. "I won't have anything illegal going on in my motel."

"No, sir. There is nothing illegal."

I reached inside my coat and took out my ID and badge and showed it to him.

"I'm counting on you not to discuss what I am telling you with anyone. I'm involved in an investigation which has nothing to do with you, or your motel, or any of your staff. I do not wish to use my real name for two reasons. The first is, I don't want to bring any attention to your motel, or you and your staff. Secondly, I don't want anyone to know that I am here. I wish to spend a quiet night here, and leave quietly in the morning. By registering under an assumed name, no one will know I'm here unless you tell them, plus, there will not be a trail to where I am by using a credit card."

"I understand, Mr. McCord."

"It's Mr. van Hunt."

"Yes sir. If you will pay me in cash, I'll get you a receipt. You will not have to deal with my desk clerk who will have to have some kind of ID to show her if you pay in cash."

"Fine."

I reached in my wallet and got out more than enough cash to cover the cost of the room. I handed it to him.

"Keep the change," I said with a smile.

"Yes, sir."

The man looked at the money I gave him. He smiled then looked at me.

"Thank you, sir."

I knew I had given him a good size tip, but it was worth it to have privacy.

"You're welcome."

"I'll get you a receipt."

"In the name of van Hunt. Remember, I want nothing to show I was here."

"Yes, sir."

I watched him as he walked back to his office. He returned in a matter of just a few minutes. He handed me my receipt and key to a room. I thanked him, then went to my room. The room was very nice, typical of most motels that are well maintained. I was sure it was one of the better rooms in this little out of the way motel. I was also sure that the big tip didn't hurt, either.

I set down my luggage, then sat down at the desk and made a call to Wilma van Hunt. It was answered on the second ring.

"Hi. How's it going?"

"Slow. Did you run a complete financial report on Franklin P. Stevenson? He is a judge in Chicago."

"Yes, I did. I have it right here. I haven't looked at it yet."

"Take a look at it now. I want to know if he is living beyond his means, where he spends his money and where he gets his money?"

"Okay. Give me a minute."

I waited while she looked over the report she had on Stevenson.

"His credit report shows that he doesn't owe very much. He has several credit cards, all with fairly large balances on them. His only loan is for his rather large home in an affluent Chicago suburb. The loan is for less than most middle-class people have on a much smaller house. Oh, there is a loan on a 1932 Duesenberg."

"I thought he inherited it from his father?"

"He might have, but he has put a lot of money into it. With the amount he put into it, it would be my guess that he had the car restored.

"I guess that is not going to get me anywhere."

"A check on his financial records shows a little different story. I see here that he had invested a great deal of money in the purchase of some kind of stock, but the company went belly up. He apparently lost everything, and I mean everything, except his job as a judge."

"When did this happen?"

"Just over five years ago. In fact, he was flat broke five years ago. He almost lost his house, but, - - Wow."

"What did you find?"

"It shows that he was suddenly able to pay off almost all his debts. He must have come into a rather large sum of money."

"How did that happen?"

"It doesn't say here. It also shows that he inherited the Duesenberg about that same time, but doesn't show who from. Maybe he inherited a good chunk of money, too," Monica said.

"I guess that is possible. I was hoping to find something I could use to pressure him a little."

"Wait."

"Did you find something else?"

"Maybe. I have my doubts that he inherited anything. His father died eleven years before he got all this money and the car. His father lived in a small town in the Midwest and ran a small grocery store there. It was the only grocery store in the town."

"Where did you get that information?"

"I ran a background check on his father. It came up showing me when his father died, and a little about his family. Franklin was an only child and worked his way through college working in a grocery store near where he went to college. Franklin came from a family that didn't really have much," Monica said.

"Then where did the money come from?"

"It doesn't say. It just suddenly showed up. There's no indication at all on where it came from."

"Where was Stevenson when he came into all that money?"

"He was a judge in Chicago at the time. He's been on the bench a long time. He's not far from retirement."

"I've got an idea where it came from. What happened at, or very shortly before, he came into the money in Chicago? By that, I mean, what cases did he preside over just before he came into all that money?"

"Give me a minute. I'll see what I can find," Monica said.

I had no doubt that she knew what I had in mind.

"I think I have what you are looking for. It seems that Stoker's son, Mark, went to trial in front of Judge Stevenson for murdering a man in a bar. Mark Stoker got off when the judge, Stevenson, admonished the prosecutor for misconduct and called a mistrial. I don't see any of the details here, except for the fact that the prosecutor was apparently so mad that he resigned and left Chicago. The case was never brought to trial again. End result was Mark got off scot free."

"Good work. I think that might explain how Judge Stevenson came into so much money so quickly. I think that is what I was looking for. It sure looks as if he was paid off by William Stoker for getting his son out from under a murder charge. There's little doubt in my mind that Judge Stevenson is dirty. See if you can find out what happened to the prosecutor. I might like to talk to him."

"I'll look him up."

While I waited, I thought about how I was going to use this information.

"I got it. Oh, I'm afraid this will not help you much."

"Why is that?"

"The prosecutor's name was Harold Townsend. He moved to St Paul, Minnesota, shortly after Mark Stoker's trial, where he died of an accidental gunshot wound while hunting in the woods in northern Minnesota."

"When did he die?" I asked.

"It looks like in the fall after the trial. Do you think he was murdered so he wouldn't be a problem for Stoker in the future?"

"I'd almost be willing to bet on it. When did he resign and move to Minnesota?"

"Shortly after the trial was over, that would have been in April. He died only about six or seven months after the trail."

"I have a feeling about that," I said.

"I think you are right. He was probably murdered," Monica said.

"Townsend was probably murdered to keep him from testifying if the case against Mark ever came up again. It appears as if Stoker would do anything to protect him and his family from any kind of assault on him or his family, including murder."

"Oh, wait. There's something else here. It seems the local county sheriff has issued an arrest warrant for Mark Stoker on suspicion of the murder of Harold Townsend. It seems they found something that caused them to look into Townsend's death with an eye toward murder."

"I'm not surprised. Are there any other details?"

"All it says here is that the death of Townsend was suspicious."

"Okay. That was some good work."

"Thank you. What are you going to do now?"

"I'm going to get a good night's sleep. Tomorrow, I'm going to pay Franklin P. Stevenson a visit at his office."

"You be careful," Monica said.

"I will. I love you."

"I love you, too."

After a few minutes of talking about us and nothing about the investigation, I said goodnight and hung up. I decided that it was best if I get some well needed rest. Tomorrow could be very interesting.

I took a shower, then went to bed. It took me awhile to get to sleep. I had a lot to think about.

I woke the next morning to the sound of thunder. I was getting ready to head out when the phone began to ring. I reached out and picked up the receiver.

"Hello?"

"Mr. van Hunt, this is the manager."

"Yes, what is it?"

"A local police officer stopped in a little while ago asking about a Nick McCord."

"What did you tell him?"

"I told him that we didn't have anyone registered here by that name. He asked to see my registration cards. I showed him the cards. He made a comment on the card showing Randolph van Hunt."

"What did he say?"

"He thought it was a strange name. I told him that you were probably from Canada, or possibly England, and that I knew some van Hunts from Canada. When he said there wasn't a car with Canadian plates on it in the lot, I told him that it was probably because you were driving a rental car."

"That was good thinking. What did he do then?"

"He said I was probably right, then left."

"Is he still hanging around?"

"No, sir. He got in his patrol car and left."

"Thanks for your help. I will be leaving soon. By the way, from what you said, I take it he was a patrol officer, not a detective."

"Yes sir. He was a regular patrolman. I've seen him around several times."

"Thanks again. You can check me out. I'll be leaving in a few minutes."

"Yes, sir. Thank you for staying with us."

"You're welcome, and I'll remember your motel." I said then hung up.

I had to think about what just happened. I wondered if the patrol officer would be watching the place, or if he was just out checking motels looking for me. Since I was not in Chicago, the local police might have gotten a call from the Chicago police to check to see if I was staying in their community.

I picked up my luggage and walked to a side exit from the motel. Looking out the small window in the door, I didn't see anything that should concern me. I left the motel, put my luggage in the car and drove out onto the street.

I headed back to Chicago. I knew where I was likely to find Judge Stevenson's office. It would be in the courthouse.

Traffic was fairly heavy at this early hour with people going from the suburbs to their place of employment in Chicago. It was sprinkling a little, but it didn't seem to slow anyone down. The traffic moved along at a pretty good pace until we got closer to the inner-city. From then on, it was bumper to bumper.

CHAPTER TWENTY-FOUR

I arrived in Chicago at about eight in the morning. By the time I found the courthouse that dealt with criminal cases, it was close to nine. It took me the better part of thirty minutes to find a parking place.

Knowing that I would have to clear through security as soon as I entered the building, I took my badge and gun and locked them in a metal lockbox in the trunk before going into the building.

I entered the building and walked up to the metal detector. After putting my pen, coins, wallet and belt buckle on the conveyor, I walked through the metal detector. Once I cleared, I gathered my belongings and proceeded to the elevators. I checked the directory next to the elevators.

The offices of Judge Franklin P. Stevenson were on the fourth floor. I took the elevator to the fourth floor. It didn't take me long to find his office.

When I entered the office, I was greeted by a woman who was probably in her mid-to-late-fifties. She looked up at me, but didn't smile.

"Can I help you," she asked.

The tone of her voice didn't convey any real interest in helping me. In fact, her look and the tone of her voice conveyed a total lack of interest in why I was disturbing her. I had no idea what I disturbed her from doing because she was just sitting at her desk.

"I would like to speak with Judge Franklin P. Stevenson, if he is available?'

"You cannot speak with him right now. He is in session at the moment."

"When do you think he might be available for me to talk to him?"

"That is hard to say. What is it you wish to talk to him about?"

"It is rather personal, and very important to him that I talk to him as soon as possible."

"It will be some time before I can even interrupt him to tell him you are here."

"Since it is important enough that I talk to him as soon as possible, I will wait here, if you don't mind."

"Suit yourself," she said rather sharply.

I wasn't sure if she was just having a bad day, or if she was always this inhospitable. From the expression on her face, I was sure that she had not had very many people who would simply sit down and wait to see the judge.

I looked around the room and saw a couple of chairs with a small table between them in a corner. I walked over, sat down on a chair and picked up a magazine from the table. I made myself as comfortable as possible and tried to look as if I was settling in for a long stay, which I was if it was necessary to see the judge.

She didn't say anything, but I noticed that she would glance over at me every few minutes. I think I was making her nervous by just sitting there and not paying any attention to what she was doing. It was my hope that she would become more and more nervous the longer I sat there. Maybe she would become so nervous that she would tell Judge Stevenson I was there and wanted to talk to him.

I doubted that she would call security to get them to remove me from the office since I wasn't doing anything that should bother her. I was not interrupting her busy day, although she didn't look like she was doing anything but pushing papers around on her desk. I certainly was within my rights to wait to see the judge.

It was almost noon when she stood up and went through a door behind her desk. I was sure it led to the office of Judge Stevenson. A quick look at my watch showed me that court would probably recess for lunch at almost any time now.

It wasn't very long before she came back out. She walked up to me.

"Judge Stevenson would like to know what you want."

"It is a personal matter that concerns him, or at the very least should concern him."

She looked at me for a minute before she turned around and went back to the judge's office. It was only a couple of minutes before she returned.

"He wants to know who you are."

"I'm a private investigator. My name is Nick McCord, and I am from Madison, Wisconsin."

"If you're from Wisconsin, you don't have any jurisdiction here," she reminded me rather sharply.

"That is where you are wrong. I'm also licensed in Illinois, as well as in several other states."

She looked at me for a moment without saying a word. It was a good thing that she didn't ask me to show her my badge, however, I could show her my ID. I thought about it, but I decided not to offer to show it to her.

She simply turned around and went into the judge's office. She returned in about two or three minutes.

"Judge Stevenson will see you."

I stood up and followed her to the door. She held the door while I entered the judge's chamber. When she left, she didn't close the door completely. I reached back and shut the door myself. What I had to say to the judge was certainly none of her business.

"What is it you find so important as to interrupt my lunchtime?"

"My name is - - - ."

"I already know your name. What is it you want?" Judge Stevenson said rather sharply.

"I want to talk to you about murder, several murders in fact. All of them are related to a very long time and personal friend of yours," I said as I sat down in front of his desk.

"What are you talking about, and who is this friend of mind you think is involved in these - murders?"

"The friend I am referring to is William F. Stoker."

He stared at me. His body language showed he was suddenly very interested in what I might have to say.

"I know Mr. Stoker."

"You more than just know him, Your Honor."

"What is that supposed to mean?"

"It means you are on the same board of trustees at one of the local golf courses, you have shown your antique automobile at several shows with him, you are a member of the same antique auto club, and you are in business with him."

From his body language, he was thinking very hard about what I had said.

"I'm in business with him? What are you talking about? I'm not in business with anyone."

"Yes, you are. Your company is W.S. and S., and it is located in the Cayman Islands, offshore as some like to say. Of course, I know it to be nothing but a shell company."

The look on his face told me that he was fast getting concerned with what I knew, or might know about him and Stoker. Since he didn't comment, I continued.

"I also know that you presided over the murder trial of Mark Stoker, that would be Mr. Stoker's son. Mark was accused of murdering a man in a bar. In fact, he beat the man to death."

"That is a matter of public record," he said.

"Yes, it is, but you should have recused yourself from presiding over it because of your close relationship to his father, but you didn't. Instead, you belittled the prosecutor, unjustly I might add, then let Mark off by declaring a mistrial."

"That's not true."

"Yes, it is true. It is also a matter of public record. Your belittling of the deputy DA was uncalled for based on court records of the trial. You knew the prosecutor had a good solid case, but you dumped it without cause."

"He was sloppy."

The judge's comment didn't sound very convincing.

"The DA who prosecuted Mark Stoker had a case that was cut and dried. Mark Stoker should have been jailed for a very long time, at the very least."

The judge just sat there looking at me. From the look on his face, and his body language, I got the impression that he was not only very concerned about how much I knew, but how much of it I could prove.

"Do you happen to know where Stoker's son, Mark, is now?"

"No. Why would I know that?"

"He is in the Cayman Islands," I said.

On this point I was guessing. I had no idea where Mark Stoker was, but the Cayman Islands seemed a likely spot, especially if he knew there were arrest warrants out on him in Illinois as well as in Minnesota. It would be my guess that his father knows about the arrest warrants, and probably hustled his son off to the Cayman Islands where he would be out of reach of the U.S. courts. There was also the fact that William Stoker had a rather large home in the Caymans.

I gave the judge a moment to let that soak in. I could see that he was starting to sweat. It was time to press on.

"I also know that William Stoker, and most likely you, have been involved in buying off Brandon Smith's company in Calumet City, a little bit at a time over the past couple of years."

"So, what. It was a plain and simple business deal. My only involvement in it was as an investor. If this is all you have, you're wasting my time."

Judge Stevenson stood up expecting me to stand up and leave, but I didn't move.

"Sit down, judge. I'm not finished."

I waited as he looked at me. I wasn't sure what he was going to do. He could call security and have me thrown out, but I didn't think he would do that without first finding out just how much I really knew about him and his activities. Suddenly, without a word, he sat back down.

"That was a wise decision. Now to continue. There are three people dead, murdered in fact. All of them connected to Stoker. I know that Stoker did not kill them himself, but I also know that the men who did kill them are employed by Stoker. People working for Stoker don't even breath without Stoker's permission, but I'm sure you know that."

"What are you trying to say?"

The look on his face and the nervousness of his voice showed me that he was scared to death. I wasn't sure if it was because of me and the fact that I knew so much, or because he knew that Stoker would not hesitate to kill him to keep him from talking.

It also told me that he was in this up to his neck even if he had nothing to do with the murders. I knew that I had his undivided attention.

"A few years ago, you were the judge in a case involving Stoker's son."

"You already said that."

"Yes, I did. I happen to know, and can prove, that you were in debt up to your eyeballs when that case started. You were so far in debt that you were about to lose your house and car. As soon as you declared a mistrial, you had enough money to pay off all your debts, buy a 1932 Duesenberg roadster and have it completely restored. You paid cash for the restoration of the car."

I gave him a minute to let that all soak in. He was really beginning to sweat now. Judge Stevenson had to be thinking that I knew everything there was to know about him, and his less than legal activities. My knowing that scared the hell out of him.

"I want your help in putting William F. Stoker away for the rest of his life. If you need some time to think over what I've said so far, I will wait until the end of this day's session is over."

"Then what?"

"I'm sure you know that your life as a judge is over. What you do to help me and the police put Stoker away will determine to a great degree what happens to you."

I watched him as he looked down at his hands resting on the top of his desk. He had a lot to think about. I gave him time to think about what I had told him. After a few minutes, he looked up at me but didn't speak right away.

"I - - - I guess - - I should cancel the afternoon session," he said after taking a deep breath.

"I would think that would be a good idea. I wouldn't try to call Stoker if I were you. He has already tried to get rid of me. Besides, my partner has all the information on you and Stoker, as well as all the others involved. He would be very quick to turn it over to the federal authorities if anything happens to me."

"Are you trying to blackmail me?"

Although he was scared to death, his anger at the idea of blackmail showed on his face.

"Not at all. I'm simply telling you that your reputation and your life of freedom is about to come to a very quick end. Only your help will decide how much of a life of freedom you will have when this is over."

He slouched in his fancy leather chair. I could see by the look on his face that he knew it was over for him.

"Ah - - You can wait here while I go into the outer office, Mr. McCord."

I watched him as he stood up.

"I wouldn't try to run if I were you. There's no place to go. And if you run, you will not have just the police looking for you, but Stoker as well."

"I'm not going to run. I'll be back in a few minutes."

I nodded then watched him as he stepped out into the outer office. It was easy to hear what he said to his secretary because he left the door open just a little. It was probably so I would know that he wasn't going to try to leave.

"Miss Jenkins, would you be so kind as to contact council for both sides and tell them that court will be postponed until ten o'clock tomorrow morning. I have something very important to take care of this afternoon."

"Is everything okay?"

"Yes. Everything is fine. Something very important has come up. Oh, you may take the rest of the day off as soon as you have notified councils about the delay in the trial. I will not be here this afternoon."

"But, - - - ."

"Please do as I say, Miss Jenkins."

"Yes, sir."

It was only a matter of a minute or so after he finished talking to her when I heard the front office door open and then close. I was sure his secretary had left the office. I doubted that he would try to run, even if he only believed half of what I told him.

Judge Franklin P. Stevenson returned to his office. He walked around behind his desk and almost slumped down in his chair. He sat there for a minute looking around the room before he spoke.

"What do we do now?" he asked. "It's obvious my career is over."

"Is there anyone at your house?"

"No. Well, yes. I have a housekeeper living at my house."

"I want you to go home. On your way home, I want you to stop and pick up a cell phone. Don't call anyone, and don't let anyone see you. Once you get home, I want you to stay out of sight."

"I can't just disappear."

"You better if you want to live very long."

"My career is over. I'll be going to jail."

"That may be true, but you might be able to get off with a short sentence if you cooperate with the DA. If you cooperate with the DA, and don't give either of us any trouble, I will put in a good word for you."

"Okay. How will I get in touch with you?"

"You can call me on the cell phone you buy on your way home. As soon as you get the cell phone, activate it. Then call this number and let me know what your new phone number is," I said as I handed him one of my cards. "Don't call anyone else on the new cell phone. Don't call on your home phones, and don't even answer your home phone. Your life depends on you doing as I say. I'm sure you know that Stoker will not hesitate to kill you if he thinks for one minute that you talked to me or the DA."

"What about my housekeeper? She lives there and often answers my phone."

"Can you get her out of the house for a few days?"

"I don't know. She lives there."

"Okay. She is to tell anyone who comes to the house or calls, that you left town to visit an old friend in - - -."

"In Wisconsin? I have a friend that lives there."

"Okay, in Wisconsin. That your friend is dying of cancer. She doesn't expect you back until Monday. That way you won't have to take more than, two days off from your office. Just Thursday and Friday."

"What happens then?"

"I will have time to arrange for you to be protected. I'll also have time to talk to the DA. I'm sure he will be as lenient as he possibly can if you cooperate with him. There is little doubt that he would like nothing more than to get Stoker and his goons put away. I happen to know he has been trying to do just that for a long time, and it would be a feather in his cap, so to speak, to shut Stoker down."

"Okay. I'll do what you say. I only hope it works."

"I'll keep my end. You have to keep yours. Remember, no one must know where you are. You are to do nothing that will indicate that you are in your home. Be careful about what lights you have on at night. Make sure you don't go into any rooms that someone can see in. And most of all, if anyone comes to your door make sure you hide in a place where you will not be found."

"I understand."

"Oh, one more thing. I want you to write down everything you can think of that Stoker has done that was illegal, what your relationship to him is, and everything else that you know first-hand about him. Also, gather any and all documents you might have to support his illegal activities."

"I'll do my best."

"Okay. Now, get out of here. Go home and don't talk to anyone. If Miss Jenkins should call you, or come to your home, do not talk to her or see her."

"I'll go out the back way."

"Do it now."

"What are you going to do?"

"I'm going to talk to the DA."

He nodded that he understood. I watched him grab his hat and leave the office. I only hoped that he would do what I had told him to do.

As soon as he was gone, I walked out of his office. By using the front door to his office, it put me in a different hall. I walked to the elevators and took one down to the lobby of the building. I cleared through security, then went to my car. I got my gun and badge from the trunk of the car, then I drove directly to the DA's office.

CHAPTER TWENTY-FIVE

I arrived at the DA's office shortly after one in the afternoon. After showing the woman sitting at the desk in the front office my badge and ID, I handed her one of my business cards. I told her that I wanted to see the DA and that it was very important.

The woman took my business card, stood up and went into the DA's office. It was only a matter of a few minutes before she returned.

"Mr. Walter Simmons will see you," she said with a smile.

I followed her into the office of the DA. DA Simmons stood up and walked around in front of his desk and stuck his hand out. I shook his hand.

"Mr. McCord, I have heard good things about you. What can I do for you?"

"Well sir, I'll get right to the point. I happen to know that it has been very hard for you to get any information on the activities of one William F. Stoker that will help you get him behind bars. I might be able to help you with that problem."

"I see you are as good an investigator as I have heard. You are right about not being able to get much incriminating information on Stoker. It seems he wiggles out of everything we have had on him. What does your visit to my office have to do with Stoker, and how do you think you can help?"

"I have an individual who has very close ties to Stoker. He is someone who is in a position to know a lot about Stoker's activities, both legal and illegal. And, he is willing to talk."

"Who is this person?"

"It is Judge Franklin P. Stevenson."

"You're kidding?"

"No, sir. I am not kidding."

"Do you know where he is now?"

"Yes, sir."

"I'll get some men over there to pick him up."

"Not so fast, sir."

"Why? What's the problem?"

"Stoker has a well-organized operation. It would be my guess that he has a few law officers on his payroll. I wouldn't want the wrong people to get ahold of the judge."

"Do you know this for a fact?" Simmons asked.

"No, sir, but think about it. Every time you have arrested him in the past, he has gotten off, and in several cases, released without any future action taken because the witness is found dead, or refuses to testify, or vital evidence has suddenly disappeared."

"That is true. Since you came to me, you must think that you have a way to make sure Judge Stevenson will not be killed while in the custody of the police, is that right?"

"Something like that," I said.

"Okay. What do you suggest?"

"First of all, I'll have Judge Stevenson picked up by the U.S. Marshals and placed in protective custody. It shouldn't be too hard since Stoker is also wanted by the U.S. Marshals.

"The judge has witnessed many of Stoker's activities and is willing to talk. He will be able to show that Stoker committed crimes in several states, making it a Federal case. Stoker would very likely be charged in Federal Court."

"We can protect him here," Simmons insisted.

"I doubt that. I'm sure he has ways of getting out. How many times have you had witnesses that didn't show up, or were found dead, or you had evidence disappear?"

"I see you're point. Everything we have tried in the past has failed for one or more of those reasons."

"I have a friend of mine on the Chicago Police Department. I would like to have him select a few good men that he knows well enough to know that they will do a good job of making raids on Stoker's home and office, or any place else where Stoker might have incriminating records. In the meantime, I'll have the U.S. Marshals go to where I have the judge hidden."

"Okay. You can contact this officer and have him get his men together."

"Good. It will take me awhile to get the men together. I will let you know when we are ready to attack Stoker at his home and office," I said.

"In the meantime, I would like you to see if you can find out where Stoker is so he can be arrested as quickly and quietly as possible. I don't want to raid his home and office only to find out that he is on the golf course. If that should happen, he could get away.

"I don't know if you know this, but he has a place in the Cayman Islands. I don't want him to be able to get there," I said.

"I understand. I'll find out where he is. I'll have my men ready to make our move on him as soon as you call," Simmons said.

"Good. I'll have my friend get his group ready by five p.m. I'll have his group ready to attack Stoker's office and his home. You be ready to grab Stoker wherever he is. If he keeps his usual routine, he will be home at five. I'll let you know when to go." I said.

"We'll be ready. Good luck," DA Simmons said.

"Good luck to you."

I turned and left the DA's office. My next stop was the police precinct where my friend, Detective Norman Walker, worked.

I arrived at the precinct where my friend worked and knocked on the door of his office.

"Come in."

I opened the door and found Norm sitting behind his desk. He was going through some papers. He looked up to see who had come in."

"Well, where have you been?"

"I've been to the DA's office. We are going to raid Stoker's home and office."

"What are you talking about?"

"I have a witness that will put the nail in Stoker's coffin, so to speak."

"You're kidding?"

"That's what the DA said. I need you to get several good men together to attack Stoker's office and home at the same time. They have to be men you can trust not to leak out what is going to happen, and to do the job."

"I can't just get a team together on your say so, as much as I would like to."

"It's not on my 'say so'. You can call the DA if you like. He is getting a team together to help out. The DA is going to arrest Stoker at the same time you are attacking his office and home.

"We need to keep this quiet. This may be your last chance to get Stoker and his bunch. If it fails, he will probably run for the Caymans, out of our reach."

"Okay. Will you be going with us?"

"Not right now, but if all goes well, I'll be with our witness, protecting him."

"Good."

"I have to go now. I'll be calling you when we are ready."

"I'll be ready within the hour."

"Good."

I left Norm in his office and walked out to my car. I sat in the parking lot of the police precinct to place a call to the U.S. Marshal's office.

Just as I was about to call the U.S. Marshal's office, my phone began to ring.

"Hello?"

"Is this Nick McCord?"

"Yes."

"This is Stevenson. I'm at home. You told me to call as soon as I got a new phone."

"Okay, let me have the number."

I didn't say anything while I wrote down the number of his new cell phone.

"Okay. Remember what I told you. As soon as I call the U.S. Marshals, I will be coming out to your place. Do not talk to anyone, or see anyone until I get there."

"I won't. Why the U.S. Marshals?"

"They want Stoker as much or more than the DA. They are much better at protecting someone. They will be your body guards, and they're good at it."

"Okay."

"Remember what I told you? I want you to get busy writing down everything you can think of that Stoker has done that is illegal or even the least bit shady."

"I've already started."

"Good. I'll be there shortly."

As soon as I hung up, I placed a call to the U.S. Marshal's office and asked for a longtime friend of mine. He just happened to be the Marshal in Charge of that office.

"U.S. Marshal's office. How may I help you?"

"This is Nick McCord, I would like to speak to Dave Brugger, please."

"Just a minute."

It wasn't long before Dave was on the phone.

"Detective McCord, it is good to hear from you. How are you doing?"

"I'm good. I've got a little bit of a problem, though. I could use your help."

"Okay, how can I help?"

"I know that the Chicago DA has been trying to put William F. Stoker away for some time. It's my guess that you would also like to put him away."

"That is for sure. You got a way to do it, or am I asking too much?"

"You are not asking too much. I have a way to do it. I not only have a plan on how to capture him, I have an excellent witness who is willing to talk and help put him in jail."

"Okay. Is it a good solid witness?"

"The best. He knows what goes on inside the Stoker organization."

"That is music to my ears. How can I help?"

"I need you, and a couple of your agents, to meet me at Judge Franklin P. Stevenson's home. Don't make a show of getting there. In fact, I want it as low key as possible. I want you to come as soon as I call so he doesn't run. Do you understand?"

"Yeah. Is the judge your witness?"

"Yes."

"As soon as you call me, I'll come out to his place with just one other agent to help secure the place. Once we have it secured, I'll call in four other agents to make sure he is protected."

"That sounds good. I'm on my way out to Judge Stevenson's place, now."

"I'll get ready for your call."

"Thanks," I said then hung up."

I started my car and drove out of the police parking lot. Once I was out on the street, I started toward the judge's home. I kept an eye out for anyone who might be following me. I even took a couple of round-about ways to get there just to make sure I was not followed.

I arrived at Judge Stevenson's home at about four in the afternoon. After parking my car in front of the garage, I walked up to the front door and rang the bell, then waited. When no one answered the door, I rang it again. It took a couple of minutes before I heard the sound of the door being unlocked. Behind the door was an elderly woman peering out at me. She didn't say anything.

"I'm Nick McCord. I'm here to see Judge Stevenson."

"The judge is not home, and I don't know when he will return. His brother is very sick and he took some time off to visit him."

"Where does his brother live?" I asked.

I smiled to myself. She was putting on a good act.

"He lives in Wisconsin, but I don't know the name of the town."

"That was very good. I still need to talk to him."

"He isn't here," she said sharply.

"Thank you," I said.

I turned and reached for my phone. I placed a call to the number the judge had given me. It rang only twice before it was answered.

"Is that you, Mr. McCord?"

"Yes. Would you be so kind as to tell your housekeeper to let me in?"

I handed her my phone. She looked at me as if she didn't know what to do with it. She put it up to her ear and said "hello."

"Mildred, let Mr. McCord in, then shut the door and lock it."

Mildred looked at me as she handed me the phone. She then stepped back and let me into the house. I watched her as she closed and locked the door.

"Mr. McCord, come on upstairs."

I looked up the staircase. Judge Stevenson was standing at the top of the stairs. I quickly ran up the stairs, then followed him into a room that looked like it was an office. The windows had curtains on them and they were closed making the room rather dark. He walked over to a rather large desk and sat down. I walked over to the desk. There was a desk light, a pad of paper with some writing on it and a pen lying next to the pad.

"I've been making a list of all the things I can remember about Stoker's activities."

"I see. What are the little stars on some of these entries?" I asked as I looked at what he had been writing.

"Those are the items that I have documents to support."

"You have a lot of them."

"I kept records just in case this day came before I retire. I guess that day has come."

"I think it has."

"I understand why you called in the U.S. Marshals, but do you think that was a good idea?"

From the look on his face, he was worried.

"I have the U.S. Marshals involved for two reasons. The first being, they are better at protecting you. The second is, I figured you would get a better deal from them then you would from the Chicago DA."

"Will I go to a Federal Prison?"

"Maybe, maybe not. It will depend on the how much help you are in putting Stoker away. You could end up under the Witness Protection Program."

"I don't know if that is any better than prison."

"At least you will not be behind bars. They may even help you to move out of the country, but at least out of state. They will make it hard for anyone to find you. In prison, it would be pretty easy to find you."

"You do have a point there."

"I'll leave you to your work. I want to be here when the U.S. Marshals arrive."

The Judge just nodded. I turned and left the room. I walked toward the staircase. About halfway down there was a landing. I walked to the landing, then sat down on a small bench next to a window where I could look out and see most of the driveway. It was time to call the U.S. Marshals.

I called Dave and told him it was time to come to the judge's house. He told me he would be there in twenty minutes. I leaned back to wait.

CHAPTER TWENTY-SIX

I had been sitting on the small bench on the landing of the staircase for about fifteen minutes when a dark colored sedan turned off the street and started up the long curved driveway. The car moved rather slowly up the drive. I continued to watch it as it stopped in front of the house.

It seemed a little strange that the car would come up the drive so slowly. If it was Dave and his partner, Dave would have driven right up because he knew I was expecting him. As several scenarios ran through my head, I was sure that this didn't look good.

The car came to stop at the front door to the house. I could see three men get out of the car. There was supposed to be only two men if it was Dave and his partner. Dave was not one of them. The three men looked around as if they were looking to see if anyone was there. The one who looked like he was in charge motioned for one of the men to go around to the back of the house.

That was my clue that things were not going as planned. I quickly picked up my phone and called Dave. When he answered the phone, I didn't give him time to say anything.

"We are under attack. Need help now," I said then hung up and grabbed my gun from under my coat.

"Mildred, come here and hurry."

It was only a short moment when I saw her walking as fast as she could.

"Up here," I called to her. "Go down the hall and tell the judge we have company and he is to hide. You hide with him."

She looked scared, but I couldn't blame her. The good thing was she did what I told her without any discussion.

Mildred was no more than out of sight when I heard the two who had come to the front of the house try the door. When the door did not open, it didn't take them long to break in. Once they were in the house, they looked around as if trying to decide where to go. I had my gun pointed right at them.

"Hold it right there," I yelled.

They looked up at me and could see I had them covered.

"Drop the guns."

Just as they dropped their guns, a shot rang out from inside the house. That was when everything went to hell. The bullet hit the heavy maple post of the stair railing, scattering small pieces of wood all over. Several pieces hit me in the face.

I returned fire and hit one of the men at the door just as another shot hit the post. I quickly scrambled for a better place to take cover. Two shots were fired at me as I ran up the stairs. They didn't even come close. When I reached the top of the stairs, I quickly dropped to the floor near the top of the staircase. I took a position that would allow me to keep anyone from coming upstairs while keeping out of sight of those below.

The one who had come in from the back of the house must have decided that I was out of the fight. He came running around the corner and started up the stairs. He was firing as he ran up the stairs. I waited until I could see his head, then I pulled the trigger. My bullet hit him right in the head. He fell over backwards and tumbled down the stairs, ending up in a heap on the landing.

With two down, the third man fired a couple of shots toward where I was as he backed toward the front door. Just as he turned to run out the door, he stopped suddenly, dropped his gun, then put his hands up. He backed up as he looked out the door.

Just then Dave stepped inside the house followed by his partner and two other U.S Marshals. He was holding his gun on the only gunman that was still standing. Dave's partners cuffed the man and took him out of the house.

"Nick, you okay?" Dave called out as he walked toward the stairs.

"Yeah, Dave."

"Are there any others?"

"No. Just the three. The one here on the landing, and the one on the floor by the door."

"Is the judge okay."

"Yeah. He's upstairs hiding in his office."

I sat down on the step to take a minute to catch my breath. Dave and two U.S. Marshals went on by me. It wasn't but a couple of minutes before he came back to the stairs with Judge Stevenson in handcuffs. The two U.S. Marshals took Stevenson out to their car.

I picked up my phone and called DA Simmons. I told him it was time to grab Stoker. I quickly hung up and called Detective Norman Walker and told him to attack Stoker's office and home, and to secure all his files and papers. Now it was time to wait to see if they were going to find Stoker and place him under arrest.

Time passed slowly. Waiting to find out if Stoker had been arrested seemed to take forever. It wasn't long before four more U.S. Marshals showed up.

"How are you doing?" Dave asked as he sat down beside me.

"I'm okay. I'm just waiting to see if the DA and the local police got Stoker."

"The judge is being taken to my office by two of my agents. I'll have my men here to go over the house. What are you going to do now?"

"Wait and see if they get Stoker."

"Can I make a suggestion?"

"Sure."

"I would like you to drive over to the hospital and get the cut on your face taken care of."

I reached up and touched my cheek. I flinched a little when my finger touched the cut on my cheek. I smiled at Dave.

"I think that is a good idea. But before I go, can you tell me how Stoker's men knew to come here and kill the judge?"

"I had a couple of my men go to his office to make sure no one had been there and to secure any papers the judge might have there. It seems his secretary told a couple of Stoker's men that you had been talking to the judge, and that he had gone home right after you talked with him. They were coming to the house to make sure he was not going to talk to anyone again."

"I figured that was probably what happened."

"When you get done at the hospital, stop by my office and give us your statement. After that you can go home if you like. I'll call you if or when we need you. With what the Judge has said so far, and his written list of Stoker's activities, I doubt we will need you to come back for Stoker's trial."

"I'll stop by your office. I would like to know if they got Stoker."

"Okay. I'll see you later."

Before I stood up, one of Dave's marshals walked in with a big smile on his face. I waited to hear what he had to say. He walked up to Dave.

"Any news on Stoker?" Dave asked.

"Yeah, they caught him and five of his muscles. They have so many papers and files on Stoker's activities that it will take us a month to go through all of it. From what little I've been told they seem pretty damning. We also found a list of Stoker's employees. We're hunting them down now."

"Great. Well, Nick, you did a good job."

I thanked Dave for saving my butt, then left the Judge's house. I drove to a local hospital to get the injury to my cheek taken care of, then drove to Dave's office.

After a brief summary of everything that had happened, I dictated my statement about what happened at the judge's house. When I finished with my statement, I sat back to talk to Dave.

"What about Barbara Smith, what happens to her?" I asked.

"She is at her estate. With what papers we've had a chance to look at, it looks like she was not involved. She was actually a victim. She will be able to get back all her stock in the company that was sold without her knowledge.

"We did get Josh Ellis. From what the police have told us, he will be charged with killing the men who worked the gates at the Smith Estate, and the murder of Russell Larson," Dave explained. "Ellis was one of those who tampered with the car causing it to crash."

"It looks like you have it all wrapped up," I said.

"It looks that way. Thanks to you."

"In that case, I think I'll go get a motel room for the night and go home in the morning."

"Sounds like a good idea. If we have any questions, I'll give you a call."

"Okay. I'll see you around," I said.

I left Dave to finish up his investigation and drove to a motel for the night.

Once in my room at the motel, I sat down and placed a call to Barbara Smith. She said that she was pleased that I could prove it was murder, and that I helped in catching those involved. She also assured me that I would get paid as soon as I sent her a bill. She also told me that she would be opening up her husband's business at the new plant. I thanked her then hung up.

My next call was to Monica. We talked for awhile about the case. I told her how much help she had been in bringing this case to its final conclusion, at least as far as we were concerned. She got concerned when I told her I got a small cut on my cheek from a flying piece of wood. It took me a couple of minutes to convince her that it was nothing serious.

"What now," she asked.

"I thought I would come up to the lodge in the morning. We could spend a few days just relaxing and enjoying the peace and quiet."

"That sounds like a good idea. By the way, the president of the university called the other day. He left a message on our answering machine. He wants to talk to you about a job."

"He wants to talk to me about a job?"

"Yes."

"What kind of a job would the university have for me?"

"He wants you to become a professor and teach several courses in the Criminal Justice Department. It wouldn't be much different from the classes you taught at the Police Academy."

"No. Is he serious?" I asked.

"Yes. He read your book on collecting and preserving evidence at the scene of a crime, and he did a little checking up on you. You have experience teaching, as well as experience as a policeman, then as a detective and currently as a private investigator. He thinks you would be a perfect fit for the job."

"I'll have to think about it."

"While you are thinking about it, he also offered me a job in the history department. They want me back to head up the department."

I took a minute to think about it. After what happened today, it didn't sound like a bad idea. We could get out of the job as private investigators. I was pretty sure I would have fewer people shooting at me.

"I think we should discuss it when I get there," I said.

"Does that mean you will consider it?"

"It does. I love you. I'll leave from here first thing in the morning. I should be there by late afternoon.

"I can hardly wait. I guess I can shut down the computer and relax until you get here."

"You can. I love you."

"I love you, too."

I didn't want to, but I hung up the phone. It had been a long day and I needed to get some rest. I watched a little of the news. There was a story about the arrest of William F. Stoker, but I shut it off. It was time for me to forget about him. Besides, I knew the real story.

I took a shower and went to bed. It didn't take me long to get to sleep.

After a good night's sleep, I drove to Madison and left Monica's sports car at the apartment. I grabbed a cab to go to the motel where I left my Explorer.

Alfred was glad to see me. We sat down in his office where I told him about my investigation and the outcome of it. He seemed pleased that he had been able to be a part of it, even if it was a very small part.

I thanked him for his help, paid for the rooms he held for me, and for keeping my Explorer until I returned. He saw me to my Explorer and wished me well. I drove away feeling pretty good that I had made him happy by sharing my investigation with him.

When I arrived, Monica was waiting for me on the large porch that surrounded the lodge. It was raining a little just like it had been on the day I first met her.

She didn't wait for me to come onto the porch this time. She ran out to greet me. She through her arms around me and gave me a kiss like I had not had for some time.

"I'm glad you're here."

"I'm glad to be here."

"Does it hurt?" Monica asked as she looked at the dressing over the wound on my face."

I reached up and touched the dressing on my cheek.

"No. It's nothing serious."

She took my arm and led me to the porch. We sat down on the swing.

"I've had a chance to think about the job at the university. In fact, I had a long drive to think about it."

"Did you decide what you want to do. If you want to keep being a private investigator, I'm okay with that. I will work with you." Monica said.

"I think it would be a good idea if we look into it. We would both have steady jobs in the fields we like, and we would be able to have a good stable home life we talked about."

She looked at me sort of funny at the last part of my comment.

"We could raise that family we both want, and still be doing what we like. What do you think?" I asked.

"I think I love you," she said, then threw her arms around me and kissed me.

After four days at the lodge, making love, enjoying walks along the shore of Lake Michigan, discussing our future, and just being close; we returned to our apartment in Madison.

On the day after we returned to Madison, we went to the office of the President of the University and told him we would accept his offer. He suggested that we start at the beginning of next fall's semester.

Monica would be the head of the History Department, and I would head up the Criminal Justice Department. In that capacity, I would be teaching a number of police officers as well as those looking to a future in all different aspects of police work.

All was well.

www.ingramcontent.com/pod-product-compliance
Lightning Source LLC
Chambersburg PA
CBHW071149170626
46809CB00002B/825